CAPTAIN JANUARY

By

LAURA E. RICHARDS

Author of

"Melody," "Marie," "Rosin, The Beau," "The
Hildegarde-Margaret Series," "Three Minute
Stories," "Five Minute Stories," etc.

THE PAGE COMPANY

BOSTON PUBLISHERS

CAPTAIN JANUARY

Forty-ninth Impression, June, 1919

THE COLONIAL PRESS
C. H. SIMONDS CO., BOSTON, U. S. A.

CONTENTS

CAPTAIN JANUARY

CHAPTER I.

STAR BRIGHT

THE Captain had sold all his lobsters. They had been particularly fine ones, and had gone off "like hot cakes," every one who passed by the wharf stopping to buy one or two. Now the red dory was empty, and the Captain had washed her out with his usual scrupulous care, and was making preparations for his homeward voyage, when he was hailed by a cheery voice from the street.

"Hillo, January!" said the voice. "Is that you? How goes it?" and the owner of the voice, a sturdy man in a blue coat with brass buttons, came down the wharf and greeted the Captain with a hearty shake of the hand.

"How goes it?" he repeated. "I haven't seen ye for a dog's age."

"I'm hearty, Cap'n Nazro!" replied Captain Jan-

1

uary. "Hearty, that's what I am, an' hopin' you're the same."

"That's right!" said the first speaker. "'Tain't often we set eyes on you, you stick so close to your light. And the little gal, she's well, I expect? She looks a picture, when I take a squint at her through the glass sometimes. Never misses running out and shaking her apron when we go by!"

"Cap'n Nazro," said January, speaking with emphasis, "if there is a pictur in this world, o' health, and pootiness, and goodness, it's that child. It's that little un, sir. Not to be beat in this country, nor yet any other, 'cordin' as I've voyaged."

"Nice little gal!" said Captain Nazro, assenting. "Mighty nice little gal! Ain't it time she was going to school, January? My wife and I were speaking about it only the other day. Seems as if she'd oughter be round with other children now, and learning what they do. Mis Nazro would be real pleased to have her stop with us a spell, and go to school with our gals. What do you say?" He spoke very heartily, but looked doubtfully at the old man, as if hardly expecting a favourable answer.

Captain January shook his head emphatically. "You're real kind, Cap'n Nazro!" he said; "real kind, you and Mis Nazro both are! and she makin' the little un's frocks and pinafores, as is a great help. But I can't feel to let her out o' my sight, nohow; and as for school, she ain't the kind to abear it, nor yet I couldn't for her. She's learnin'!" he added, proudly. "Learnin' well! I'll bet there ain't no gal in your school knows more nor that little un does. Won'erful, the way she walks ahead!"

"Get the school readers, hey! and teach her yourself, do you?" queried Captain Nazro.

"No, sir!" replied the old man; "I don't have no school readers. The child learns out o' the two best books in the world, — the Bible, and William Shakespeare's book; them's all the books she ever seed — *saw*, I should say."

"William Shak—" began Captain Nazro; and then he broke off in sheer amazement, and said, simply, "Well, I'm blowed!"

"The minister giv 'em to me," said Captain January. "I reckon he knows. There's a dictionary, too," he added, rather sadly; "but I can't make her take to that, nohow, though there's a power o' fine words in it."

Then, as the other man remained silent and openmouthed, he said: "But I must be goin', Cap'n Nazro, sir! The little un'll be lookin' for me. Good day, sir, and thank ye kindly, all the same as if it was to be, which it ain't!" And with a friendly gesture, the old man stepped into his red dory, and rowed away with long, sturdy strokes.

Captain Nazro gazed after him meditatively, took out his pipe and looked at it, then gazed again. "January's cracked," he said; "that's what's the matter with him. He's a good man, and a good lighthouse-keeper, and he's been an able seaman in his day, none better; but he's cracked!"

There is an island off a certain part of the coast of Maine, — a little rocky island, heaped and tumbled together as if Dame Nature had shaken down a heap of stones at random from her apron, when she had finished making the larger islands which lie between it and the mainland. At one end, the shoreward end, there is a tiny cove, and a bit of silver-sand beach, with a green meadow beyond it, and a single great pine; but all the rest is rocks, rocks. At the farther end the rocks are piled high, like a castle wall, making a brave barrier against the Atlantic waves; and on top of this cairn rises the lighthouse, rugged and sturdy as the rocks themselves, but painted white, and with its windows shining like great, smooth diamonds. This is Light Island; and it was in this direction that Captain January's red dory was headed when he took his leave of his brother-captain, and rowed away from the wharf. It was a long pull; in fact, it took pretty nearly the whole afternoon, so that the evening shadows were lengthening when at length he laid down his oars, and felt the boat's nose rub against the sand of the little home-cove. But rowing was no more effort than breathing to Captain January, and it was no fatigue, but only a trifle of stiffness from sitting so long, that troubled him a little in getting out of the boat. As he stepped slowly out upon the firm-grained silver of the little beach, he looked up and around with an expectant air, and seeing no one, a look of disappointment crossed his face. He opened his lips as if to call some one, but checking himself, " Happen she's gettin' supper ! " he said. " It's later than I thought. I don't pull so spry as I used ter, 'pears ter me. Wal, thar ! 'tain't to be expected. I sh'll be forty years old before I know it ! "

Chuckling to himself, the Captain drew up the little boat and made her fast ; then, taking sundry brown-paper parcels from under the thwart, he turned and made his way up towards the light-house. A picturesque figure he was, striding along among the heaped and tumbled rocks. His hair and beard, still thick and curly, were absolutely white, as white as the foam that broke over the rocks at the cliff's foot. His face was tanned and weather-beaten to the colour of mahogany, but the features were strong and sharply cut, while the piercing blue eyes which gleamed beneath his shaggy eyebrows showed all the fire of youth, and seemed to have no part in the seventy years which had bent the tall form, and rounded slightly the broad and massive shoulders. The Captain wore a rough pea-jacket and long boots, while his head was adorned with a nondescript covering which might have begun life either as a hat or a cap, but would now hardly be owned by either family.

Reaching the house, the old man mounted the rude steps which led to tne door, and entered the room which was kitchen, dining, and drawing room at Storm Castle, as the lighthouse was called by its inhabitants. The room was light and cheerful, with a pleasant little fire crackling sociably on the hearth. The table was laid with a clean white cloth, the kettle was singing on the hob, and a little covered saucepan was simmering with an agreeable and suggestive sound; but no one was to be seen. Alarmed, he hardly knew why, at the silence and solitude, Captain January set his parcels down on the table, and going to the foot of the narrow stone staircase which wound upward beside the chimney, called, " Star! Star Bright, where are you? Is anything wrong?"

" No, Daddy Captain!" answered a clear, childish voice from above; " I'm coming in a minute. Be patient, Daddy dear!"

With a sigh of relief, Captain January retired to the fireplace, and sitting down in a huge high-backed armchair, began leisurely pulling off his great boots. One was already off and in his hand, when a slight noise made him look up. He started violently, and then, leaning back in his chair, gazed in silent amazement at the vision before him.

On the stone stairway, and slowly descending, with steps that were meant to be stately (and which might have been so, had not the stairs been so steep, and the little legs so short) was the figure of a child: a little girl about ten years old, with a face of almost startling beauty. Her hair floated like a cloud of pale gold about her shoulders; her eyes were blue, not light and keen, like the old man's, but of that soft, deep, shadowy blue that poets love to call violet. Wonderful eyes, shaded by long, curved lashes of deepest black, which fell on the soft, rose-and-ivory tinted cheek, as the child carefully picked her way down, holding up her long dress from her little feet. It was the dress which so astonished Captain January. Instead of the pink calico frock and blue checked pinafore, to which his eyes were accustomed, the little figure was clad in a robe of dark green velvet with a long train, which spread out on the staircase behind her, very much like the train of a peacock. The body, made for a grown woman, hung back loosely from her shoulders, but she had tied a scarf of gold tissue under her arms and round her waist, while from the long hanging sleeves her arms shone round and white as sculptured ivory. A strange sight, this, for a lighthouse tower on the coast of Maine! but so fair a one, that the old mariner could not take his eyes from it.

"Might be Juliet!" he muttered to himself. "Juliet, when she was a little un. 'Her beauty hangs upon the cheek o' Night,'—only it ain't, so to say, exactly night,—'like a rich jewel in a nigger's ear.' No! that ain't right. 'Nigger' ain't right, 'Ethiop's ear,' that's it! Though I should judge they were much the same thing, and they more frekently wear 'em in their noses, them as I've seen in their own country."

As he thus soliloquised, the little maiden reached the bottom of the stairs in safety, and dropping the folds of the velvet about her, made a quaint little courtesy, and said, " Here I am, Daddy Captain! how do you like me, please ? "

" Star Bright," replied Captain January, gazing fixedly at her, as he slowly drew his pipe from his pocket and lighted it. " I like you amazin'. *A*-mazin' I like you, my dear! but it is what you might call surprisin', to leave a little maid in a blue pinafore, and to come back and find a princess in gold and velvet. Yes, Pigeon Pie, you might call it surprisin', and yet not be stretchin' a p'int."

" Am I *really* like a princess ? " said the child, clapping her hands, and laughing with pleasure. " Have you ever seen a princess, Daddy Captain, and did she look like me ? "

" I seed — I *saw* — one, once," replied the Captain, gravely, puffing at his pipe. " In Africky it was, when I was fust mate to an Indiaman. And she wa'n't like you, Peach Blossom, no more than Hyperion to a Satyr, and that kind o' thing. She had on a short petticut, comin' half-way down to her knees, and a necklace, and a ring through her nose. And — "

" Where were her other clothes ? " asked the child.

" Wal — maybe she kem off in a hurry and forgot
'em!" said the Captain, charitably. " Anyhow, not
speakin' her language, I didn't ask her. And she
was as black as the ace of spades, and shinin' all over
with butter."

" Oh, *that* kind of princess!" said Star, loftily. " I
didn't mean that kind, Daddy. I meant the kind
who live in fretted palaces, with music in th' enam-
elled stones, you know, and wore clothes like these
every day."

" Wal, Honey, I never saw one of that kind, till
now!" said the Captain, meekly. " And I'm sorry I
hain't — I mean I *ain't* — got no fretted palace for
my princess to live in. This is a poor place for golden
lasses and velvet trains."

" It *isn't!* " cried the child, her face flashing into
sudden anger, and stamping her foot. " You sha'n't
call it a poor place, Daddy! It's wicked of you. And
I wouldn't live in a palace if there were *fifty* of them
all set in a row. So there now!" She folded her
arms and looked defiantly at the old man, who returned her gaze placidly, and continued to puff at his
pipe, until he was seized in a penitent embrace, hugged,
and kissed, and scolded, and wept over, all at once.

The brief tempest over, the child seated herself
comfortably on his knee, and said, " Now, Daddy, I
want a story."

" Story before supper?" asked the Captain, meekly,
looking at the saucepan, which was fairly lifting its

lid in its eagerness to be attended to. A fresh access of remorseful hugging followed.

"You poor darling!" said Star; "I forgot all about supper. And it's stewed kidneys, too! But oh! my dress!" and she glanced down at her velvet splendour. "I must go and take it off," she said, sadly.

"Not you, Honeysuckle," said the old man, rising and setting the child down carefully in the chair. "Sit you there, and be a real princess, and I will be your steward, and get supper this time. I like to see you in your fine clothes, and 'twould be a shame to take 'em off so soon."

She clapped her hands again, and settling herself cosily in the great chair, arranged her train with a graceful sweep, and pushed back her cloudy golden hair.

"Shall I really act princess?" she asked, — and without waiting for an answer, she began to give orders in lofty tones, holding her head high in the air, and pointing hither and thither with her tiny hands. "Take up the golden chafing-dish, Grumio!" she cried. "The kidneys — I mean the capons — are quite ready now. And the milk — no! the sack — is in the silver flagon!" she pointed to an ancient blue jug which stood on the dresser.

The obedient Captain hastened to take up the saucepan, and soon the frugal supper was set out, and princess and steward were doing ample justice to it.

"You didn't say 'Anon! anon! Madam' when I ordered you about," said the Princess, thoughtfully. "You ought to, you know. Servants always do in the book."

"Wal, I didn't think on't," the steward admitted. "I wa'n't brought up to the business, you see, Princess. It always seemed to me a foolish thing to say, anyhow: no disrespect to W. Shakespeare. The hull of the word's 'anonymous,' I believe, and the dictionary says *that* means 'wanting a name.' So, altogether, Star Bright, I haven't been able to make much sense out o' that answer."

"Oh, never mind!" said the Princess, tossing her head. "I don't like the dictionary. It's a wretch!"

"So 'tis, so 'tis," assented the Captain, with servile alacrity. "Have some more milk then, Sunshine."

"It isn't milk! it's sack," said the child, promptly, holding out her small yellow mug with a royal air. "Are the capons good, Grumio?"

"They are, my lamb, they are," replied the Captain. "Oncommon good they are, to be sure, and me not knowin' to this day what capons was. A little more? Yes, Pigeon Pie, I *will* take a little more, thank ye kindly."

"I don't *think*, Grumio, that you ought to call me lambs and pigeon pies just now," remarked the Princess, judiciously. "Do you think it's respectful? they don't in Shakespeare, I'm sure."

"I won't do it again, Honey — I mean Madam,"

said the Captain, bowing with great humility. "I beg your honourable majesty's pardon, and I won't never presume to —"

"Yes, you will!" cried the Princess, flinging herself across the table at him, and nearly choking him with the sudden violence of her embrace. "You shall call me pigeon pie, and anything else you like. You shall call me rye porridge, though I hate it, and it's always full of lumps. And don't ever look that way again; it *kills* me!"

The Captain quietly removed the clinging arms, and kissed them, and set the half-weeping child back in her place. "There, there, there!" he said, soothingly. "What a little tempest it is!"

"Say 'delicate Ariel,'" sobbed Star. "You haven't said it to-day, and you always say it when you love me."

"Cream Cheese from the dairy of Heaven," replied the Captain; "if I always said it when I loved you, I should be sayin' it every minute of time, as well you know. But you *are* my delicate Ariel, so you are, and there ain't nothin' in the hull book as suits you better. So!" and his supper ended, the good man turned his chair again to the fire, and took the child, once more smiling, upon his knee.

"And now, Ariel, what have you been doin' all the time I was away? Tell Daddy all about it."

Star pondered a moment, with her head on one side, and a finger hooked confidentially through the

Captain's buttonhole. "Well," she said, "I've had a *very* interesting time, Daddy Captain. First I cleaned the lamps, of course, and filled and trimmed them. And then I played Samson a good while; and —"

"And how might you play Samson?" inquired the Captain.

"With flies!" replied Star, promptly. "Heaps upon heaps, you know; ' With the jaw-bone of an ass have I slain a thousand men.' The flies were the Philistines, and I took a clam-shell for the jaw-bone; it did just as well. And I made a song out of it, to one of the tunes you whistle: ' With the jaw-bone! with the jaw-bone! with the jaw-bone of an ass!' It was very exciting."

"Must ha' been," said the Captain, dryly. "Well, Honeysuckle, what did you do then?"

"Oh, that took some time!" said the child. "And afterward I fished a little, but I didn't catch anything, 'cept an old flounder, and he winked at me so, I put him back. And then I thought a long time — oh! a very long time, sitting like Patience on the doorstep. And *suddenly*, Daddy Captain, I thought about those boxes of clothes, and how you said they would be mine when I was big. And I measured myself against the doorpost, and found that I *was very* big. I thought I must be almost as big as you, but I s'pose I'd forgotten how big you were. So I went up, and opened one box, and I was just putting the dress on when you came in. You knew where it came from, of course, Daddy, the moment you saw it."

The Captain nodded gravely, and pulled his long moustaches.

" Do you suppose my poor mamma wore it often ? " the child went on, eagerly. " Do you think she looked like me when she wore it ? Do I look as she did when you saw her ? "

" Wal," began the Captain, meditatively ; but Star ran on without waiting for an answer.

" Of course, though, she looked very different, because she was dead. You are quite very positively sure my poor mamma was dead, Daddy Captain ? "

" She were," replied the Captain, with emphasis. " She were that, Pigeon Pie ! You couldn't find no-body deader, not if you'd sarched for a week. Why, door nails, and Julius Cæsar, and things o' that description, would ha' been *lively* compared with your poor ma when I see her. Lively ! that's what they'd ha' been."

The child nodded with an air of familiar interest, wholly untinged with sadness. " I think," she said, laying her head against the old man's shoulder, and curling one arm about his neck, " I think I should like to hear about it again, please, Daddy. It's a long, long time since you told me the whole of it."

" Much as a month, I should think it must be," assented the Captain. " Why, Snowdrop, you know the story by heart, better'n I do, I believe. 'Pears to me I've told it reg'lar, once a month or so, ever since you were old enough to understand it."

"Never mind!" said the Princess, with an imperious gesture. "That makes no difference. I *want* it now!"

"Wal, wal!" said the Captain, smoothing back the golden hair. "If you *want* it, why of course you must have it, Blossom! But first I must light up, ye know. One star inside the old house, and the other atop of it: that's what makes Light Island the lightest spot in the natural world. Sit ye here, Star Bright, and play Princess till Daddy comes back!"

CHAPTER II.

THE STORY

THE lamps were lighted, and the long, level rays flashed their golden warning over the murmuring darkness of the summer sea, giving cheer to many hearts on inbound barque or schooner. Bright indeed was the star on the top of the old lighthouse; but no less radiant was the face of little Star, as she turned it eagerly towards Captain January, and waited for the beginning of the well-known and well-loved story.

"Wal," said the Captain, when his pipe was refilled and drawing bravely. "Let me see now! where shall I begin?"

"At the beginning!" said Star, promptly.

"Jes' so!" assented the old man. "Ten year ago this—"

"No! No!!" cried the child. "*That* isn't the beginning, Daddy! That's almost half-way to the middle. 'When I was a young lad.' That's the beginning."

"Bound to have it all, are ye, Honeysuckle?" said the obedient Captain. "Wal! wal! when I were a

16

young lad, I was a wild un, ye see, Treasure. My
father, he 'prenticed me to a blacksmith, being big
and strong for my years; but I hadn't no heart for
the work. All I cared about was the sea, and boats,
and sailors, and sea talk. I ran away down to the
wharf whenever I could get a chance, and left my
work. Why, even when I went to meetin', 'stead o'
listenin' to the minister, I was lookin' out the places
about them as go down to the sea in ships, ye know,
and ' that leviathan whom Thou hast made,' and all
that. And there was Hiram, King of Tyre, and his
ships! Lord! how I used to think about them ships,
and wonder how they was rigged, and how many tons
they were, and all about it. Yes! I was a wild un,
and no mistake; and after awhile I got so roused
up — after my mother died, it was, and my father
married again — that I just run away, and shipped
aboard of a whaler, bound for the north seas. Wal,
Honey, 'twould take me a week to tell ye about all
my voyages. Long and short of it, 'twas the life I
was meant for, and I done well in it. Had tumbles
and toss-ups, here and there, same as everybody has
in any kind o' life; but I done well, and by the time
I was forty year old I was captain of the *Bonito*, East
Indiaman, sailin' from New York to Calcutta."

The Captain paused, and puffed gravely at his pipe
for a few minutes.

" Well, Rosebud," he continued, presently, " you
know what comes next. The *Bonito* was cast away,

in a cyclone, on a desert island, and all hands lost, except me and one other."

" Dear Daddy! poor Daddy! " cried the child, putting her little hands up to the weather-beaten face, and drawing it down to hers. " Don't talk about that dreadful part. Go on to the next! "

" No, I won't talk about it, Star Bright! " said the old man, very gravely. " Fust place I can't, and second place it ain't fit for little maids to hear of. But I lived on that island fifteen year, — five year with my good mate Job Hotham, and ten year alone, after Job died. When a ship kem by, after that, and took me off, I'd forgot most everything, and was partly like the beasts that perish; but it kem back to me. Slow, like, and by fits, as you may say; but it kem back, all there was before, and maybe a good bit more! "

" Poor Daddy! " murmured the child again, pressing her soft cheek against the white beard. " It's all over now! Don't think of it! I am here, Daddy, loving you: loving you *all to pieces*, you know! "

The old man was silent for a few minutes, caressing the little white hands which lay like twin snowflakes in his broad, brown palm. Then he resumed, cheerfully:

" And so, Cream Cheese from the dairy of Heaven, I kem home. Your old Daddy kem home, and landed on the same wharf he'd sailed from twenty-five years before. Not direct, you understand, but takin' steamer from New York, and so on. Wal, there wa'n't nobody that knew me, or cared for me. Father was dead, and his wife; and their children, as weren't born when I sailed from home, were growed up and gone away. No, there wa'n't nobody. Wal, I tried for a spell to settle down and live like other folks, but 'twa'n't no use. I was'nt used to the life, and I couldn't stand it. For ten years I hadn't heard the sound of a human voice, and now they was buzz, buzzin' all the time; it seemed as if there was a swarm of wasps round my ears the everlastin' day. Buzz! buzz! and then clack! clack! like an everlasting mill-clapper; and folks starin' at my brown face and white hair, and askin' me foolish questions. I couldn't stand it, that was all. I heard that a light-keeper was wanted here, and I asked for the place, and got it. And that's all of the fust part, Peach Blossom."

The child drew a long breath, and her face glowed with eager anticipation. " And *now*, Daddy Captain," she said, " *now* you may say, ' Ten year ago this fall!'"

" Ten year ago this fall," said the Captain, meekly acquiescing, " on the fourteenth day of September, as ever was, I looks out from the tower, bein' a-fillin' of the lamps, and says I, ' There's a storm comin'!' So I made all taut above and below, and fastened the door, and took my glass and went out on the rocks, to see how things looked. Wal, they looked pooty bad.

There had been a heavy sea on for a couple o' days, and the clouds that was comin' up didn't look as if they was goin' to smooth it down any. There was a kind o' brassy look over everythin', and when the wind began to rise, it warn't with no nat'ral sound, but a kind of screech to it, on'arthly like. Wal, thar! the wind did rise, and it riz to stay. In half an hour it was blowin' half a gale; in an hour it blew a gale, and as tough a one (barrin' cyclones) as ever I see. 'T had like to ha' blow me off my pins, half a dozen times. Then nat'rally the sea kem up; and 'twas all creation on them rocks, now I tell ye. ' The sea, mountin' to the welkin's cheek;' ye remember, Pigeon Pie?"

The child nodded eagerly. "Tempest!" she said, "Act I., Scene 2: 'Enter Prospero and Miranda.' Go on, Daddy!"

"Wal, my Lily Flower," continued the old man. "And the storm went on. It roared, it bellowed, and it screeched: it thumped and it kerwhalloped. The great seas would come bunt up agin the rocks, as if they was bound to go right through to Jersey City, which they used to say was the end of the world. Then they'd go scoopin' back, as if they was callin' all their friends and neighbours to help; and then, bang! they'd come at it agin. The spray was flyin' in great white sheets, and whiles, it seemed as if the hull island was goin' to be swallowed up then and thar. 'Tain't nothin' but a little heap o' rocks, anyhow, to face the hull Atlantic Ocean gone mad: and on that heap o' rocks was Januarius Judkins, holdin' on for dear life, and feelin' like a hoppergrass that had got lost in Niag'ry Falls."

"Don't say that name, Daddy!" interrupted the child. "You know I don't like it. Say 'Captain January'!"

"I tell ye, Honeysuckle," said the old man, "I felt more like a sea-cook than a cap'n *that* night. A cap'n on a quarter-deck's a good thing; but a cap'n on a p'int o' rock, out to sea in a northeast gale, might just as well be a fo'c'sle hand and done with it. Wal, as I was holdin' on thar, I seed a flash to windward, as wasn't lightning; and next minute kem a sound as wasn't thunder nor yet wind nor sea."

"The guns! the guns!" cried the child, in great excitement. "The guns of my poor mamma's ship. And then you heard them again, Daddy?"

"Then I heard them agin!" the old man assented. "And agin! a flash, and a boom! and then in a minute agin, a flash and a boom! 'Oh, Lord!' says I. 'Take her by to the mainland, and put her ashore there!' I says; 'cause there's a life-saving station thar, ye know, Blossom, and there might be some chance for them as were in her. But the Lord had His views, my dear, the Lord had His views! Amen! so be it! In another minute there kem a break in the clouds, and thar she was, comin' full head on, straight for Light Island. Oh! my little Star, that was an awful thing to see. And I couldn't do nothin', you understand. Not a livin' airthly thing could I do, 'cept hide my face agin the rock I was clingin' to, and say, ' Dear Lord, take 'em easy! It's Thy will as they should be took,' I says, ' and there ain't no one to hender, if so be as they could. But take 'em easy, good Lord, and take 'em suddin ! ' "

" And He did ! " cried the child. " The good Lord did take 'em sudden, didn't He, Daddy Captain ? "

" He did, my child ! " said the old man, solemnly. " They was all home, them that was goin', in ten minutes from the time I saw the ship. You know the Roarin' Bull, as sticks his horns out o' water just to windward of us ? the cruelest rock on the coast, he is, and the treacherousest : and the ship struck him full and fair on the starboard quarter, and in ten minutes she was kindlin' wood, as ye may say. The Lord rest their souls as went down in her ! Amen ! "

" Amen ! " said little Star, softly. But she added in an eager tone, " And now, Daddy, you are coming to me ! "

" Pooty soon, Jewel Bright ! " said the old man, stroking the gold hair tenderly. " I'm a-comin' to you pooty soon. 'Twas along about eight bells when she struck, and none so dark, for the moon had risen. After the ship had gone down, I strained my eyes through the driving spray, to see whether anything was comin' ashore. Presently I seed somethin' black, driftin' towards the rocks : and lo' ye, 'twas a boat, bottom side up, and all hands gone down. Wal! wal! the Lord knew what was right: but it's wuss by a deal to *see* them things than to be in 'em yourself, to my thinkin'. Wal, after a spell I looked agin, and there was somethin' else a-driftin' looked like a spar, it did: and somethin' was lashed to it. My heart! 'twas tossed about like a egg-shell, up and down, and here and thar! 'Twas white, whatever was lashed to it, and I couldn't take my eyes off'n it. 'It can't be alive!' I says, 'whatever it is!' I says. 'But I'll get it, if it takes a leg!' I says. For down in my heart, Jewel, I knew they wouldn't ha' taken such care of anythin' *but* what was alive, and they perishin', but I didn't think it could live in such a sea long enough to get ashore. Wal, I kep' my eyes on that spar, and I see that 'twas comin' along by the south side. Then I ran, or crawled, 'cordin' as the wind allowed me, back to the shed, and got a boat-hook and a coil o' rope; and then I clumb down as far as I dared, on the south rocks. I scooched down under the lee of a p'int o' rock, and made the rope fast round my waist, and the other end round the rock, and then I waited for the spar to come along. 'Twas hard to make out anythin', for the water was all a white, bilin' churn, and the spray flyin' fit to blind you; but bimeby I co't sight of her comin' swashin' along, now up on top of a big roarer, and then scootin' down into the holler, and then up agin. I crep' out on the rocks, grippin' 'em for all I was wuth, with

the boat-hook under my arm. The wind screeched
and clawed at me like a wildcat in a caniption fit, but
I hadn't been through those cyclones for nothin.' I
lay down flat and wriggled myself out to the edge,
and thar I waited."

"And the waves were breaking over you all the
time?" cried the child, with eager inquiry.

"Wal, they was that, Honeysuckle!" said the Captain. "Bless ye, I sh'd ha' been washed off like a
log if 't hadn't ben for the rope. But that held;
'twas a good one, and tied with a bowline, and it held.
Wal, I lay thar, and all to wunst I see her comin' by
like a flash, close to me. 'Now!' says I, 'ef ther's
any stuff in you, J. Judkins, let's see it!' says I.
And I chucks myself over the side o' the rock and
grabs her with the boat-hook, and hauls her in. 'All
together,' I says. 'Now, my hearties! Yo heave
ho!' and I hed her up, and hauled her over the rocks
and round under the lee of the p'int, before I stopped
to breathe. How did I do it? Don't ask me, Jewel
Bright! I don't know how I did it. There's times
when a man has strength given to him, seemin'ly,
over and above human strength. 'Twas like as if the
Lord ketched holt and helped me: maybe He did,
seein' what 'twas I was doing. Maybe He did!" He
paused a moment in thought, but Star was impatient.

"Well, Daddy!" she cried. "And then you looked
and found it was — go on, Daddy dear!"

"I looked," continued the old man, "and I found

it was a sail, that had showed so white against the spar; a sail, wrapped tight round somethin'. I cut the ropes, and pulled away the canvas and a tarpaulin that was inside that; and thar I seed — "

"My poor mamma and me!" cried the child, joyously, clapping her hands. "Oh, Daddy Captain, it *is* so delightful when you come to this part! And my poor mamma was dead? You are quite positively sure that she was dead, Daddy?"

"She were, my lamb!" replied the Captain, gravely. "You needn't never have no doubt about it. She had had a blow on the head, your poor ma had, from one o' the bull's horns, likely; and I'll warrant she never knowed anythin' after it, poor lady! She was wrapped in a great fur cloak, the same as you have on your bed in winter, Blossom: and lyin' all clost and warm in her cold arms, that held on still, though the life was gone out of 'em, was " — the old man faltered, and brushed his rough hand across his eyes — "was a — a little baby. Asleep, it seemed to be, all curled up like a rose on its mother's breast, and its pooty eyes tight shut. I loosed the poor arms — they was like a stattoo's, so round and white and cold; and I took the child up in my arms; and lo' ye! it opened its eyes and looked straight at me and laughed."

"And it said, Daddy?" cried the delighted child, clapping her hands. "Tell what it said!"

"It said ''Tar,'" the old man continued, in a hushed voice. "''Tar,' it said as plain as I say it to you. 'And "Star" it is!' says I; for 'if ever a star shone on a dark night, it's you, my pooty,' I says. 'Praise the Lord,' I says. 'Amen, so be it.' Then I laid your poor ma in a corner, under the lee of the big rock, where the spray wouldn't fly over her, and I covered her with the sail; and then I took the fur cloak, seein' the baby needed it and she didn't, and wrapped it round the little un, and clumb back over the rocks, up to the house. And so, Honeysuckle —"

"And so," cried the child, taking his two great hands and putting them softly together, "so I came to be your little Star!"

"To be my little Star!" assented the old man, stooping to kiss the golden head.

"Your light and your joy!" exclaimed the child, laughing with pleasure.

"My light and my joy!" said the old man, solemnly. "A light from heaven to shine in a dark place, and the Lord's message to a sinful man."

He was silent for a little, looking earnestly into the child's radiant face. Presently, "You've been happy, Star Bright?" he asked. "You haven't missed nothin'?"

Star opened wide eyes of surprise at him. "Of course I've been happy!" she said. "Why shouldn't I be?"

"You ain't — I mean you haven't mourned for

your poor ma, have ye, Jewel?" He was still looking curiously at her, and his look puzzled her.

"No," she said, after a pause. "Of course not.
I never knew my poor mamma. Why should I
mourn for her? She is in heaven, and I am very
glad. You say heaven is much nicer than here, so
it must be pleasanter for my poor mamma; and
I don't need her, because I have you, Daddy. But
go on, now, please, Daddy dear. 'Next day'—"

"Next day," resumed the obedient Captain, "the
sky was bright and clear, and only the heavy sea,
and your poor ma, and you, Peach Blossom, to tell
what had happened, so far as I seed at fust. Bimeby,
when I went out to look, I found other things."

"My poor papa!" said Star, with an air of great
satisfaction.

The Captain nodded. "Yer poor pa," he said,
"and two others with him. How did I know he
was your poor pa? Along of his havin' your poor
ma's pictur hung round his neck. And a fine-lookin'
man he was, to be sure!"

"And his name was 'H. M.'!" cried the child,
eagerly.

"Them was the letters of it!" assented the Captain. "Worked on his shirt and hank'cher, so fine
as ever was. Well, Jewel Bright, when I seed all
this, I says, 'January,' says I, 'here's Christian
corpses, and they must have Christian burial!' I
says. So I brought 'em all up to the house, and

laid 'em comfortable; and then I gave you a good drink of warm milk (you'd been sleepin' like a little angil, and only waked up to smile and crow and say ' 'Tar '), and gave you a bright spoon to play with; and then I rowed over to shore to fetch the minister and the crowner, and everybody else as was proper. You don't care about this part, Honeysuckle, and you ain't no need to, but everything was done decent and Christian, and your parents and the other two laid peaceful under the big pine-tree. Then the minister, when 'twas all done, he says to me, ' And now, my friend,' he says, ' I'll relieve you of the child, as would be a care to you, and I can find some one to take charge of it!' he says. ' Meanin' no disrespect, Minister,' I says, ' don't think it! The Lord has His views, you'll allow, most times, and He had 'em when He sent the child here. He could have sent her ashore by the station jest as easy,' I says, ' if so be't had seemed best; but He sent her to me,' I says, ' and I'll keep her.' ' But how can you bring up a child?' he says, ' alone, here on a rock in the ocean?' he says. ' I've been thinking that over, Minister,' I says, ' ever since I holt that little un in my arms, takin' her from her dead mother's breast,' I says; ' and I can't see that there's more than three things needed to bring up a child, — the Lord's help, common sense, and a cow. The last two I hev, and the fust is likely to be round when a man asks for it!' I says. So then we shakes hands, and he doesn't say nothin' more, 'cept to pray a blessin' for me and for the child. And the blessin' kem, and the blessin' stayed, Star Bright; and there's the end of the story, my maid.

"And now it's time these two eyes were shut, and only the top star shinin' in the old tower. Good night, Jewel! Good night, and God bless you!"

CHAPTER III.

INTRODUCING IMOGEN AND BOB

"IMOGEN!" said Star, looking up from her book, "I don't believe you have been listening!"

Imogen looked up meekly, but made no attempt to deny the charge.

"You *must* listen!" said the child, sternly. "First place, it's beautiful: and besides, it's very rude not to listen when people reads. And you ought *not* to be rude, Imogen!" After which short lecture, Star turned to her book again,—a great book it was, lying open on the little pink calico lap,—and went on reading, in her clear childish voice:

> "'Over hill, over dale,
>   Thorough bush, thorough brier,
> Over park, over pale,
>   Thorough flood, thorough fire,
> I do wander everywhere,
> Swifter than the moony sphere;
> And I serve the fairy queen,
> To dew her orbs upon the green:'

Do you know what a fairy is, Imogen?" asked Star, looking up again suddenly.

But this time it was very evident that Imogen (who was, in truth, a large white cow, with a bell round her neck) was paying no attention whatever to the reading; for she had fairly turned her back, and was leisurely cropping the short grass, swaying her tail in a comfortable and reflective manner the while.

Star sprang to her feet, and seizing the delinquent's horns, shook them with all her might.

"How dare you turn your back when I am reading?" she cried. "I'm just ashamed of you! You're a disgrace to me, Imogen. Why, you are as ignorant as a — as — as a lobster! and you a great cow with four whole legs. A — a — ah! shame on you!"

Imogen rubbed her head deprecatingly against the small pink shoulder, and uttered a soft and apologetic "moo;" but Star was not ready to be mollified yet.

"And you know it's my *own* book, too!" she continued, reproachfully. "My own Willum Shakespeare, that I love more — well, no! not *more* than I love you, Imogen, but just as much, and almost nearly half as much as I love Daddy Captain.

"But after all," she added, with a smile flitting over her frowning little face, "after all, you poor dear, you *are* only a cow, and I don't suppose you know." And then she hugged Imogen, and blew a little into one of her ears, to make her wink it, and the two were very friendly again.

"Perhaps you would like to know, Imogen," said

Star, confidentially, seating herself once more on the ground, "*why* I am so fond of Willum Shakespeare. So I will tell you. It is really part of *my* story, but Daddy Captain didn't get as far as that last night, so I think I will tell it to you. Well!" she drew a long breath of enjoyment, and, clasping her hands round her knees, settled herself for a "good talk."

"Well, Imogen: you see, at first I was a little baby, and didn't know anything at all. But by and by I began to grow big, and then Daddy Captain said to himself, 'Here's a child,' he says, 'and a child of gentlefolks, and she mustn't grow up in ignorance, and me doing my duty by her poor pa and ma,' he says. So he rows over to the town, and he goes to the minister (the same minister who came over here before), and he says, 'Good morning, Minister!' and the minister shakes him by the hand hearty, and says, 'Why, Captain January!' he says, 'I'm amazing glad to see you. And how is the child?' And Daddy says, 'The child is a-growing with the flowers,' he says; 'and she's a-growing like the flowers. Show me a rose that's as sweet and as well growed as that child,' he says, 'and I'll give you my head, Minister.' That's the way Daddy talks, you know, Imogen. And then he told the minister how he didn't want the child (that was me, of course) to grow up in ignorance, and how he wanted to teach me. And the minister asked him was he qualified to teach. 'Not yet, I ain't!' says Daddy Captain, 'but I'm a-going to be. I want a book, or maybe a couple of books, that'll edicate me in a manner all round!' he says. 'I couldn't do with a lot of 'em,' he says, ''cause I ain't used to it, and it makes things go round inside my head. But I think I could tackle two if they was fustrate,' he says. The minister laughed, and told Daddy he wanted a good deal. Then he asked him if he had the Good Book. That's the Bible, you know, Imogen. Daddy Captain won't let me read that to you, because you are a beast that perish. Poor dear!" she leaned forward and kissed Imogen's pink nose. "And Daddy said *of course* he had that, only the letters weren't so clear as they used to be, somehow, perhaps along of getting wet in his weskit pocket, being he carried it along always. So the minister gave him a *new big* BEAUTIFUL Bible, Imogen! It isn't so new *now*, but it's just as big and beautiful, and I love it. And then he thought for a long time, the minister did, walking about the room and looking at all the books. The whole room was full of books, Daddy says, all on shelves, 'cept some on the floor and the table and the chairs. It made his head go round dreadful to see them all, Daddy says (I mean Daddy's head), and think of anybody reading them. He says he doesn't see how in creation the minister manages to keep his bearings, and look out for a change in the wind, and things that *have* to be done, and read all those books too. *Well!*" she kissed Imogen's nose again, from sheer enjoyment, and threw her head back with a laugh of delight. "I'm coming to it now, Imogen!" she cried. "At last the minister took down a big book — OH! you precious old thing, how I love you!" (this apostrophe was addressed to the quarto volume which she was now hugging rapturously), "and said, 'Well, Captain January, here's the best book in the world, *next* to the Good Book!' he says. 'You'll take this,' he says, 'as my gift to you and the child; and with these two books to guide you, the child's edication won't go far wrong!' he says; and then he gave Daddy the dictionary, too, Imogen; but I sha'n't tell you about that, because it's a brute, and I hate and 'spise it. But — well! *so*, you see, *that* was the way I got my Willum Shakespeare, my joy and my pride, my — "

At this moment a shadow fell upon the grass, and a deep, gruff voice was heard, saying, "Star, ahoy!" The child started up, and turned to meet the new-comer with a joyous smile. "Why, Bob!" she cried, seizing one of his hands in both of hers, and dancing round and round him. "Where did you come from? Why aren't you on the boat?"

"Boat's aground!" replied the person addressed as Bob. He spoke in short, jerky sentences. He was dressed as a seafaring man; had wide, helpless-look-ing brown eyes, an apologetic smile, and a bass voice of appalling depth and power. "Boat's aground," he repeated, seating himself on the grass and looking

about for a stem of grass long enough to put in his
mouth. "Hard and fast. Waiting for tide to turn;
thought I'd come, pass time o' day."

"And how came you to run her aground?" inquired the child, severely. "A pretty pilot you are!
Why, I could steer her myself better than that."

"Fog!" replied the man, in a meek and muffled
roar. Then finding a bit of sorrel, he fell upon it
with avidity, and seemed to think he had said
enough.

"H'm!" said Star, with a disdainful little sniff.
"You'd better get Daddy to steer your boat. *He*
doesn't mind fog. Are there many people on board?"
she added, with an air of interest.

"Heaps!" replied Bob, succinctly. Then, after a
pause of meditative chewing: "Like to go aboard?
take ye — boat — Cap'n willin'."

"No, I don't want to go aboard, thank you!" said
Star. "I don't like people. But you might just row
me round her once, Bob," she added. "I think I
should like *that*. But we must wait till Daddy comes,
of course."

"Cap'n round?" inquired Bob.

"He's setting the lobster-pots," replied the child.
"He'll be back soon. Bob," she added, irrelevantly,
a moment after, "I never noticed before that you
looked like Imogen. Why, you are the very image
of her, Bob! Your eyes and your expression are
exactly the same."

Bob raised his eyes and surveyed Imogen with a critical air. " Fine cow ! " he said at last. " D'no's I mind — 'f she doosn't."

" *Isn't* she a fine cow ? " cried little Star, patting the meek and graceful head of her favourite. " I don't believe there's another such cow in the world. I *know* there isn't ! I think," she added, " I will take a little ride on her, while we are waiting for Daddy Captain. Will you put me up, please, Bob ? "

The obedient Bob lifted her as if she were a ball of thistle-down, and set her on the broad back of the good cow, who straightway began to pace sedately along the bit of meadow, following the guidance of the small hands which clasped her horns. Ah ! who will paint me that picture, as my mind's eye sees it ? The blue of sky and sea, the ripples breaking in silver on silver sand, the jewelled green, where the late dandelions flecked the grass with gold ; and in the midst the lovely, laughing child, mounted on the white cow, tossing her cloudy golden hair, and looking back with eyes of delight towards her companion.

The beauty of it all filled the eyes and the heart of Captain January, as he came up among the rocks. He paused, and stood for some time in silence, watching the little well-beloved figure. " Wal ! " he said, " if that ain't one of the young-eyed cherubims, then I never seed one, that's all."

At this moment Star caught sight of him. " O Daddy," she cried. " My Daddy Captain, I'm having such a fine ride! It isn't *quite* as high as a heaven-kissing hill, but it's a heaven-kissing cow, for Imogen is really *very* high. Dear Daddy, won't you come and try it? there's plenty of room!"

"Thanky, Peach Blossom!" said the Captain, advancing, and greeting the apologetic Bob with a hearty shake of the hand. "Thanky kindly, but I don't believe I will try it. Ridin' was never, so as to say, in my line. I'm stiddy enough on my own pins, but defend me from tryin' to git about on another critter's. And how's all with you, Bob? and why ain't you aboard the *Huntress?*"

Bob in the fewest possible words related the mishap which had befallen the boat, and asked if he might take Missy out to see her.

"To be sure! to be sure!" said Captain January. "That'll be a nice trip for ye, Honeysuckle. Put on your bunnit and go with Bob. He'll take good care of ye, Bob will."

And so, by what seemed the merest chance, that lovely afternoon, little Star went with Bob Peet, in his old black boat, to see the steamer *Huntress* aground on a sand-bank off the main shore.

The sea lay all shining and dimpling in the afternoon light, and not a cloud was to be seen overhead. Here and there a white gull was slowly waving his wings through the clear air, and little fish came popping their heads out of the water, just for the pleasure of popping them back again. Star dipped her hands in the blue crystal below, and sang little snatches of song, being light of heart and without a care in the world. They were no nursery songs that she sang, for she considered herself to have outgrown the very few Mother Goose ditties which Captain January had treasured in his mind and heart ever since his mother sang them to him, all the many years ago. She was tired of

> "Jacky Barber's coming to town :
>   Clear away, gentlemen ! clear away, gentlemen !
>   One foot up and t'other foot down,
>   Jacky Barber's coming to town."

But she loved the scraps of sea-song that the old Captain still hummed over his work : "Baltimore," and "Blow a Man Down," and half a dozen other salt-water ditties : and it might have been strange to less accustomed ears than Bob Peet's to hear the sweet child-voice carolling merrily :

> "Boney was a warrior,
>   Weigh ! heigh ! oh !
>   Boney was a warrior,
>   John François !
>   Boney whipped the Rooshians,
>   Weigh ! heigh ! oh !
>   Boney whipped the Prooshians,
>   John François !
>   Boney went to Elba,
>   Weigh ! heigh ! oh !" etc.

Bob's oars kept time with the song, and his portentous voice thundered out the refrain with an energy which shook the little skiff from stem to stern. By the time that "Boney" was safely consigned to his grave in sunny France, they were nearing the flats on which the steamer *Huntress* lay, quietly awaiting the turn of the tide.

Star knew the great white boat well, for twice a day she went thundering past Light Island, churning the quiet blue water into foam with her huge paddles, on her way to and from the gay summer city which all the world came to visit. Nearly every day the child would run out on the south rocks to wave a greeting to some of her acquaintances among the crew; for she knew them all, from the black-bearded captain down to the tiniest cabin-boy; and they, for their part, were always eager — good souls! — for a smile or a nod from the "Star of Light Island." Not a man of them but envied Bob Peet his privilege of going when he pleased to the lighthouse rock. For Captain January was not fond of visitors, and gave them no encouragement to come, Bob Peet being the single exception to the rule. The Captain liked Bob because he was not "given to clatter," and "knew how to belay his jaw."

"I do love to see a man belay his jaw!" said Captain January, unconsciously quoting the words of another and a more famous captain, the beloved David Dodd. So Bob was free to come and go as he liked, and to smoke his pipe in sociable silence for hours at a time, within the walls of Storm Castle.

"Stop here, Bob!" said Star, with an imperious motion of her hand. "I don't want to go any nearer." The obedient Bob lay on his oars, and both looked up at the great boat, now only a few yards away. The decks were crowded with passengers, who leaned over the railings, idly chatting, or watching the water to see if the tide had turned.

"Sight o' folks," said Bob Peet, nodding towards the after-deck, which seemed a solid mass of human beings.

"Yes," said the child, speaking half to herself, in a low tone. "It's just like the Tower of Babel, isn't it? I should think they would be afraid. 'And the Lord scattered them abroad from thence upon the face of all the earth.' And it's so *stupid!*" she added, after a moment's pause. "Why don't they stay at home? Haven't they any homes to stay at? Who takes care of their homes while they go sailing about like loons?"

"Folks likes to v'yage," said Bob Peet, with mild toleration. "Heaps — nothin' t' do — hot spells — v'yages." He added, with an approach to a twinkle in his meek and cow-like eyes, "Try it — some day — git tired of ol' Cap'n — ol' rock — pooty soon — take ye — v'yage — "

His speech was interrupted by a sudden and violent dash of water in his face.

"Take that!" cried Star, panting with fury, and flinging the water at him with all her small might. "I wish it was sharp stones, instead of just water. I wish it was needles, and jagged rocks, and quills upon the fretful porkypine, so I do! How dare you say such things to me, Bob Peet? How dare you?" She paused, breathless, but with flashing eyes and burning cheeks; while Bob meekly mopped his face and head with a red cotton handkerchief, and shook the water from his ears, eyeing her the while with humble and deprecatory looks.

"No offence," he muttered, in apologetic thunder-rumble. "Poor ol' Bob — eh, Missy? Sorry, beg pardon! Never no more. Didn't mean it — nohow!"

The tempest subsided as suddenly as it rose, and Star, with a forgiving nod, took out her own little handkerchief and daintily wiped a few drops from her victim's forehead.

"You're so stupid, Bob," she said, frankly, "that I suppose I ought not to get angry with you, any more than I would with Imogen, though even she provokes me sometimes. So I forgive you, Bob. But if you ever say such a thing again as my getting tired of Daddy, I'll kill you. So now you know!"

"Jes' so!" assented Bob. "Nat'rally! *To* b' sure!"

The sudden splashing of the water had caught many eyes on the deck of the *Huntress*, and people admired the "playfulness" of the pretty child in the little boat. One pair of eyes, however, was sharper than the rest.

"Just look at that child, Isabel!" said a tall, bronzed gentleman who was leaning over the taff-rail. "She is a perfect little fury! I never saw a pair of eyes flash so. Very fine eyes they are, too. A very beautiful child. Isabel! why, my dear, what is the matter? You are ill — faint! let me — "

But the lady at his side pushed his arm away, and leaned forward, her eyes fixed upon Star's face.

"George," she said, in a low, trembling voice, "I want to know who that child is. I *must* know, George! Find out for me, dear, please!"

As she spoke, she made a sign towards the boat, so earnest, so imperative, that it caught Star's wandering gaze. Their eyes met, and the little child in the pink calico frock, and the stately lady in the India shawl, gazed at each other as if they saw nothing else in the world. The gentleman looked from one to the other in amazement.

"Isabel!" he whispered, "the child looks like you. What can this mean?"

But little Star, in the old black boat, cried, "Take me away, Bob! take me home to my Daddy Captain! *Quick!* do you hear?"

"Jes' so!" said Bob Peet. "Nat'rally!"

CHAPTER IV.

THE VISIT

A GRAY day! soft gray sky, like the breast of a dove; sheeny gray sea, with gleams of steel running across; trailing skirts of mist shutting off the mainland, leaving Light Island alone with the ocean; the white tower gleaming spectral among the folding mists; the dark pine-tree pointing a sombre finger to heaven; the wet, black rocks, from which the tide had gone down, huddling together in fantastic groups as if to hide their nakedness.

On the little beach two men were slowly pacing up and down, up and down, one silent, the other talking earnestly. Old men, both, with white, reverend hair: one slender and small, the other a son of Anak, big and brawny, — Captain January and the minister.

It was the minister who had been speaking. But now he had done, and they took a few turns in silence before the Captain spoke in reply.

"Minister," he said, — and his voice was strangely altered from the gruff, hearty tone which had greeted his guest fifteen minutes before. "Minister, I ain't a man that's used to hearin' much talk, and it confuses my mind a bit. There's things inside my head that seems to go round and round, sometimes, and put me out. Now, if it isn't askin' too much, I'll git you to go over them p'ints again. Slow, like! slow, Minister, bearin' in mind that I'm a slow man, and not used to it. This — this lady, she come to your house yisterday, as ever was?"

"Yesterday," assented the minister; and his voice had a tender, almost compassionate tone, as if he were speaking to a child.

"And a fine day it were!" said Captain January. "Wind steady, sou'west by sou'. Fog in the mornin', and Bob Peet run the *Huntress* aground on the bank. I never liked fog, Minister! 'Give me a gale,' I'd say, 'or anythin' short of a cyclone,' I'd say, 'but don't give me fog!' and see now, how it's come about! But it lifted, soon as the harm were done. It lifted, and as fine a day as ever you see."

The minister looked at him in some alarm, but the old man's keen blue eyes were clear and intelligent, and met his gaze openly.

"You're thinkin' I'm crazy, minister, or maybe drunk," he said, quietly; "but I ain't neither one. I'm on'y takin' it by and large. When a man has been fifteen year on a desert island, ye see, he learns to take things by and large. But I never see good come of a fog yet. Amen! so be it! And so Cap'n Nazro brought the lady to your house, Minister?"

" Captain Nazro came with her," said the minister,
" and also her husband, Mr. Morton, and Robert Peet,
the pilot.   Mrs. Morton had seen little Star in Peet's
boat, and was greatly and painfully struck by the
child's likeness to a beloved sister of hers, who had,
it was supposed, perished at sea, with her husband
and infant child, some ten years ago."

" Ten year ago," repeated Captain January, passing
his hand across his weather-beaten face, which looked
older, somehow, than it was wont to do.   " Ten year
ago this September.   'He holdeth the waters in the
hollow of His hand.'   Go on, Minister.   The lady
thought my little Star, as the Lord dropped out of
the hollow of His hand into my arms ten year ago,
had a look of her sister."

" She was so strongly impressed by it," the minister continued, quietly, " that, failing to attract Peet's
attention as he rowed away, she sent for the captain,
and begged him to give her all the information he
could about the child.   What she heard moved her
so deeply that she became convinced of the child's
identity with her sister's lost infant.   As soon as Peet
returned after putting Star ashore, she questioned
him even more closely.   He, good fellow, refused to
commit himself to anything which he fancied you
might not like, but he told her of my having per-
formed the last rites over the mortal remains of the
child's parents, and Mr. Morton wisely counselled her
to go at once to me, instead of coming here, as she

at first wished to do. After my interview with her, I am bound to say — "

" Easy now, Minister ! " interrupted Captain January. " I'm an old man, though I never knowed it till this day. Easy with this part ! "

" I am bound to say," continued the minister, laying his hand kindly on his companion's arm, " that I think there is little doubt of Star's being Mrs. Morton's niece."

" And what if she be ? " exclaimed the old sailor, turning with a sudden violence which made the gentle minister start back in alarm. " What if she be ? what have the lady done for her niece ? Did she take her out o' the sea, as raged like all the devils let loose, and death itself a-hangin' round and fairly howlin' for that child ? did she stand on that rock, blind and deef and e'ena'most mazed with the beatin' and roarin' and onearthly screechin' all round, and take that child from its dead mother's breast, and vow to the Lord, as helped in savin' it, to do as should be done by it ? Has she prayed, and worked, and sweat, and laid awake nights, for fear that child's fingers should ache, this ten years past ? Has she — " the old man's voice, which had been ringing out like a trumpet, broke off suddenly. The angry fire died out of his blue eyes, and he bowed his head humbly. " I ask yer pardon, Minister ! " he said, quietly, after a pause. " I humbly ask yer pardon. I had forgotten the Lord, ye see, for all I was talkin' about Him so glib.

I was takin' my view, and forgettin' that the Lord
had His. *He* takes things by and large, and nat'rally
He takes 'em larger than mortal man kin do. Amen!
so be it!" He took off his battered hat, and stood
motionless for a few moments, with bent head: nor
was his the only silent prayer that went up from the
little gray beach to the gray heaven above.

"Well, Minister," he said, presently, in a calm and
even cheerful voice, "and so that bein' all clear to
your mind, the lady have sent you to take my —
to take her niece — the little lady (and a lady she
were from her cradle) back to her. Is that the way
it stands?"

"Oh, no! no indeed!" cried the kind old minister.
"Mrs. Morton would do nothing so cruel as that,
Captain January. She is very kind-hearted, and fully
appreciates all that you have done for the little girl.
But she naturally wants to see the child, and to do
whatever is for her best advantage."

"For the child's advantage. That's it!" repeated
Captain January. "That's somethin' to hold on by.
Go on, Minister!"

"So she begged me to come over alone," continued
the minister, "to — to prepare your mind, and give
you time to think the matter well over. And she
and Mr. Morton were to follow in the course of an
hour, in Robert Peet's boat. He is a very singular
fellow, that Peet!" added the good man, shaking his
head. "Do you think he is quite in his right mind?

He has taken the most inveterate dislike to Mr. and Mrs. Morton, and positively refuses to speak to either of them. I could hardly prevail upon him to bring them over here, and yet he fell into a strange fury when I spoke of getting some one else to bring them. He — he is quite safe, I suppose?"

"Wal, yes!" replied Captain January, with a half smile. "Bob's safe, if any one is. Old Bob! so he doosn't like them, eh?"

At that moment his eye caught something, and he said, in an altered voice, "Here's Bob's boat coming now, Minister, and the lady and gentleman in her."

"They must have come much more rapidly than I did," said the minister, "and yet my boy rows well enough. Compose yourself, January! this is a heavy blow for you, my good friend. Compose yourself! Things are strangely ordered in this world. 'We see through a glass darkly'!"

"Not meanin' to set my betters right, Minister," said Captain January, "I never seed as it made any difference whether a man seed or not, darkly or how-sumdever, so long as the Lord made *His* views clear. And He's makin' 'em!" he added. "He's makin' 'em, Minister! Amen! so be it!" And quietly and courteously, ten minutes later, he was bidding his visitors welcome to Light Island, as if it were a kingdom, and he the crownless monarch of it. "It's a poor place, Lady!" he said, with a certain stately humility, as he helped Mrs. Morton out of the boat.

"Good anchorage for a shipwrecked mariner like me, but no place for ladies or — or them as belongs to ladies."

"O Captain January!" cried Mrs. Morton, who was a tall, fair woman, with eyes like Star's own. "What shall I say to you? I must seem to you so cruel, so heartless, to come and ask for the child whom you have loved and cared for so long. For that is what I have come for! I must speak frankly, now that I see your kind, honest face. I have come to take my sister's child, for it is my duty to do so." She laid both hands on the old man's arm, and looked up in his face with pleading, tearful eyes.

But Captain January's face did not move as he answered, quietly, "It is your duty, Lady. No question o' that, to my mind or any. But," he added, with a wistful look, "I'll ask ye to do it easy, Lady. It'll be sudden like for the — for the young lady. And — she ain't used to bein' took sudden, my ways bein' in a manner slow. You'll happen find her a little quick, Lady, in her ways, she bein' used to a person as was in a manner slow, and havin' to be quick for two, so to say. But it's the sparkle o' gold, Lady, and a glint o' diamonds."

But the lady was weeping, and could not answer; so Captain January turned to her husband, who met him with a warm grasp of the hand, and a few hearty and kindly words.

"And now I'll leave ye with the minister for a

minute, Lady and Gentleman," the Captain said; "for Bob Peet is a-signallin' me as if he'd sprung aleak below the water line, and all hands goin' to the bottom."

Bob, who had withdrawn a few paces after beaching his boat, was indeed making frantic demonstrations to attract the Captain's attention, dancing and snapping his fingers, and contorting his features in strange and hideous fashion.

"Well, Bob," said the old man, walking up to him, "what's up with you, and why are ye h'istin' and lowerin' your jib in that onarthly fashion?"

Bob Peet seized him by the arm, and led him away up the beach. "Cap'n," he said, looking round to make sure that they were out of hearing of the others, "I can't touch a lady — not seamanly! But 'f you say the word — knock gen'l'm'n feller — middle o' next week. Say the word, Cap'n! Good's a meal o' vittles t' me — h'ist him over cliff!"

CHAPTER V.

AND where was little Star, while all this was going on down on the beach? Oh, she had been having a delightful afternoon. It was cloudy, and Daddy was going to be busy, so she had determined to spend an hour or so in her own room, and enjoy all the delights of "dressing up." For the great chest that had been washed ashore from the wreck, the day after she herself had come to the island, was full of clothes belonging to her "poor mamma;" and as we have seen, the little woman was fully inclined to make use of them.

Beautiful clothes they were; rich silks and velvets, with here and there cloudy laces and strange webs of Eastern gauze. For she had been a beautiful woman, this poor mamma, and it had been the delight of Hugh Maynard, her proud and fond husband, to deck his lovely wife in all rare and precious stuffs. Some of them were stained with sea-water, and many of the softer stuffs were crumpled and matted hopelessly, but that mattered little to Star. Her eyes delighted in soft, rich colours, and she was never weary of turning them over and over, trying them on, and "playing s'pose" with them.

"S'pose," she would say, "my poor mamma was going to a banquet, like the Capulet one, or Macbeth's. Oh, no! 'cause that would have been horrid, with ghosts and daggers and things. S'pose it was the Capulets! Then she would put on this pink silk. Isn't it pretty, and soft, and creamy? Just like the wild roses on the south side of the meadow, that I made a wreath of for Imogen on her birthday. Dear Imogen! it was *so* becoming to her. Well, so my poor mamma put it on — *so!* and then she paced through the hall, and all the lords turned round and said, 'Mark'st thou yon lady?' 'Cause she was so beautiful, you know. *This* is the way she paced!" and then the little creature would fall to pacing up and down the room, dragging the voluminous pink folds behind her, her head thrown back, and a look of delighted pride lighting up her small face.

It was the funniest little place, this room of Star's, the queerest, quaintest little elfin bower! It was built out from the south side of the tower, almost like a swallow's nest, only a swallow's nest has no window looking out on the blue sea. There was a little white bed in a corner, and a neat chest of drawers, and a wash-stand, all made by Captain January's skilful hands, and all shining and spotless. The bare floor was shining too, and so was the little looking-glass which hung upon the wall.

And beside the looking-glass, and above it, and in fact all over the walls, were trophies and wonders of all kinds and descriptions. There was the starfish with ten legs, pinned up in sprawling scarlet; and there, beside him, the king of all the sea-urchins, resplendent with green and purple horns. And here were ropes of shells, and branches of coral, and over the bed a great shining star, made of the delicate gold-shells. That was Daddy's present to her on her last birthday. Dear Daddy! There, sitting in the corner, was Mrs. Neptune, the doll which Captain January had carved out of a piece of fine wood that had drifted ashore after a storm. Her eyes were tiny black snail-shells, her hair was of brown sea-moss, very thick and soft ("though as for combing it," said Star, "it is im-*possible!*"), and a smooth pink shell was set in either cheek, "to make a blush." Mrs. Neptune was somewhat battered, as Star was in the habit of knocking her head against the wall when she was in a passion; but she maintained her gravity of demeanour, and always sat with her back perfectly straight, and with an air of protest against everything in general.

In the window stood the great chest, at once a treasure-chamber and a seat; and over it hung one of the most precious things of Star's little world. It was a string of cocoanut-shells. Fifteen of them there were, and each one was covered with curious and delicate carving, and each one meant a whole year of a man's life. "For the nuts was ripe when we kem ashore, my good mate Job Hotham and me, on that island. So when the nuts was ripe agin, ye see, Jewel Bright, we knowed 'twas a year since we kem. So I took my jack-knife and carved this first shell, as a kind o' token, ye know, and not thinkin' there'd be so many to carve." So the first shell was all covered with ships: fair vessels, with sails all set, and smooth seas rippling beneath them, — the ships that were even then on their way to rescue the two castaways. And the second was carved with anchors, the sign of hope, and with coils of rope, and nautical instruments, and things familiar to seamen's eyes. But the third was carved with stars, and sickle-curved moons, and broad-rayed suns, "Because, ye see, Peach Blossom, arthly hope bein' as ye might say foundered, them things, and what was above 'em, stayed where they was; and it stiddied a man's mind to think on 'em, and to make a note on 'em as fur as might be." And then came one covered with flowers and berries, and another with fruits, and another with shells, and so on through the whole fifteen. They hung now in little Star's window, a strange and piteous record; and every night before the child said her prayers, she kissed the first and last shell, and then prayed that Daddy Captain might forget the "dreadful time," and never, never think about it again.

So, on this gray day, when other things were going on out-of-doors, Star was having a "good time" in

her room. She had found in the treasure-chest a
short mantle of gold-coloured velvet, which made
" a just exactly skirt " for her, the two ends trailing
behind enough to give her a sense of dignity, but not
enough to impede her movements. " For I am not
a princess to-day ! " she said ; " I am delicate Ariel,
and the long ones get round my feet so I can't run."
Then came a long web of what she called " sunshine,"
and really it might have been woven of sunbeams, so
airy-light was the silken gauze of the fabric. This
my lady had wound round and round her small person with considerable art, the fringed ends hanging
from either shoulder, and making, to her mind, a fair
substitute for wings. " See ! " she cried, running to
and fro, and glancing backward as she ran. " They
wave ! they really do wave ! Look, Mrs. Neptune !
aren't they lovely ? But you are envious, and that
is why you look so cross. ' Merrily, merrily, shall I
live now, under the blossom that hangs on the
bough.' " She leaped and danced about the room,
light and radiant as a creature of another world :
then stopped, to survey with frowning brows her
little blue stockings and stout laced boots. " Ariel
never wore such things as those ! " she declared ; " if
you say she did, Mrs. Neptune, you show your ignorance, and that is all I have to say to you." Off
came the shoes and stockings, and the little white
feet were certainly much prettier to look at. " Now,"
cried Star, " I will go down-stairs and wait for Daddy

Captain, and perhaps he will think I am a real fairy. Oh, wouldn't that be fun? I am *sure* I look like one!" and down the stairs she flitted like a golden butterfly. Once in the kitchen, the housewife in her triumphed for a moment over the fairy: she raked up the fire, put on more wood, and swept the hearth daintily. " But Ariel did such things for Prospero," she said. " I'm Ariel just the same, so I may as well fill the kettle and put some apples down to roast." This was soon done, and clapping her hands with delight the " tricksy spirit " began to dance and frolic anew.

> " ' Come unto these yellow sands,
>   And then take hands ! ' "

she sang, holding out her hands to invisible companions.

> " ' Courtesied when ye have, and kissed
>   (The wild waves whist !)
> Foot it featly here and there.'

" Oh! foot it featly, and feat it footly, and dance and sing, and tootle-ty ting!" cried the child, as she flitted like a golden cloud about the room. Then, as she whirled round and faced the door, she stopped short. Her arms fell by her side, and she stood as if spellbound, looking at the lady who stood in the doorway.

The lady made no motion at first, but only gazed

at her with loving and tender eyes. She was a beautiful lady, and her eyes were soft and blue, with a look of tears in them. But there was no answering softness in the starry eyes of the child : only a wide, wild look of wonder, of anger, perhaps of fear. Presently the lady, still silent, raised both hands, and kissed them tenderly to the child ; then laid them on her breast, and then held them out to her with a gesture of loving appeal.

"I don't know whether you are a spirit of health or a goblin damned," said Star; "but anyhow it isn't polite to come into people's houses without knocking, *I* think. I knowed you were a spirit when you looked at me yesterday, if you *did* have a red shawl on."

"How did you know that I was a spirit?" asked the lady softly. "Oh, little Star, how did you know?"

"'Cause you looked like my poor mamma's picture," replied the child, "that my poor papa had round his neck. Are you my mamma's spirit?"

The lady shook her head. "No, darling," she said, "I am no spirit. But I have come to see you, little Star, and to tell you something. Will you not let me come in, Sweetheart?"

Star blushed, and hung her head for a moment, remembering Captain January's lessons on politeness and "quarter-deck manners." She brought a chair at once, and in a more gracious tone said (mindful of

Willum Shakespeare's lords and ladies), " I pray you sit ! "

The lady sat down, and taking the child's hand, drew her gently towards her. " Were you playing fairy, dear ? " she asked, smoothing back the golden hair with loving touch.

Star nodded. " I was delicate Ariel," she said. " I was footing it featly, you know, on these yellow sands. Sometimes I am Puck, and sometimes Titania ; but Daddy likes Ariel best, and so do I. Did you ever play it ? " she asked, looking up into the kindly face that bent over her.

The lady smiled and shook her head. " No, dear child," she said, still with that motherly touch of the hand on the fair head. " I never thought of such a pretty play as that, but I was very happy as a child playing with my — with my sister. I had a dear, dear sister, Star. Would you like to hear about her ? "

" Yes," said Star, with wondering eyes. " Was she a little girl ? "

" Such a lovely little girl ! " said the lady. " Her hair was dark, but her eyes were like yours, Star, blue and soft. We played together always as children, and we grew up together, two loving, happy girls. Then my sister married : and by and by, dear, she had a little baby. A sweet little girl baby, and she named it Isabel, after me."

" I was a little girl baby, too," said Star, " but I wasn't named anything ; I came so : just Star."

"Little Isabel had another name," said the lady. "Her other name was Maynard, because that was her father's name. Her father was Hugh Maynard. Have you ever seen or heard that name, my child?"

Star shook her head. "No!" she said; "my poor papa's name was H. M. It was marked on his shirt and han'k'chief, Daddy says. And my poor mamma's name was Helena, just like Helena in 'Mid-summer Night's Dream.'" The motherly hand trembled, and the lady's voice faltered as she said, "Star, my dear sister's name was Helena, too. Is not that strange, my little one?"

The child looked curiously at her. "Where is your dear sister?" she asked. "Why do you cry when you say her name? is she naughty?"

"Listen, Star," said the lady, wiping the tears from her eyes, and striving to speak composedly. "My sister made a voyage to Europe, with her husband and her little baby. They spent the summer travelling in beautiful countries; and in the autumn, in September, Star, ten years ago this very year, — think of it, my dear! — they sailed for home. They came in a sailing-vessel, because the sea-voyage was thought good for your — for my sister. And — and — the vessel was never heard from. There was a terrible storm and many vessels were lost in it."

"Just like my poor mamma's ship," said the child. "Perhaps it was the same storm. Do you think — why do you look at me so?" she cried, breaking off suddenly.

But the lady put both arms round her and drew her close, close, while her tears fell fast on the golden hair. "My darling!" she cried, "my dear, dear little one! It *was* the same storm; the same storm and the same ship. Your poor mamma was my own sweet sister Helena, and you are my niece, my little Isabel, my own, own little namesake. Will you love me, darling? will you love your Aunt Isabel, and let her care for you and cherish you as your sweet mother would have done?"

Star stood very still, neither returning nor repelling the lady's caresses. She was pale, and her breath came short and quick, but otherwise she showed no sign of agitation. Presently she put up her hand and stroked the lady's cheek gently. "Why do you cry?" she asked, quietly. "My poor mamma is in heaven. Don't you like her to be in heaven? Daddy says it is much nicer than here, and he knows."

Mrs. Morton checked her tears, and smiled tenderly in the little wondering face. "Dear child!" she said, "I do like to have her in heaven, and I will not cry any more. But you have not told me whether you will love me, Star. Will you try, dear? and will you let me call you my little Isabel?"

"I will love you," replied the child, "if Daddy Captain loves you; I will love you very much. But you must not call me that name, 'cause I'm not *it*. I am just Star. *Does* Daddy love you?" she asked; and then, with a sudden note of anxiety in her voice, she exclaimed, "Where is Daddy? Where is my Daddy Captain? Did you see him when you came in?"

Her question was answered by the sound of voices outside; and the next moment the minister appeared, followed by Mr. Morton and Captain January. The old Captain hastened to place a chair for each of the gentlemen by the fireside, and then took his stand against the wall on the further side of the room. He held his weather-beaten cap in his hand, and turned it slowly round and round, considering it attentively. It might have been observed by one quick to notice trifles, that he did not look at the child, though no slightest motion of hers was lost upon him.

"George," said Mrs. Morton, joyously, to her husband, "here is our little niece, dearest Helena's child. She is going to love me, she says, and she will love you, too. Star, my darling, this is your Uncle George. Will you not give him a kiss, and be his little girl as well as mine? We have two little girls at home, and you shall be the third."

Star went obediently to Mr. Morton, who kissed her warmly, and tried to take her on his knee. "You are taller than our Grace," he said, "but I don't believe you are as heavy, my dear. Grace is just your age, and I am sure you will be great friends."

But Star slipped quietly from his arms, and, running to the Captain, took one of his hands in both of hers and kissed it. " I am Daddy Captain's little girl!" she said, looking round bravely at the others. " Why do you talk as if I belonged to you?" Then seeing the trouble in Mrs. Morton's face, she added, " I *will* love you, truly I will, and I will call you Aunt Isabel; but I cannot belong to different people, 'cause I'm only just one. Just Captain January's Star."

She looked up in the old man's face with shining eyes, but no tender, confident look returned her glance. The brown hand trembled between her two little white palms; the keen blue eyes were still bent fixedly upon the old woollen cap, as if studying its texture; but it was in a quiet and soothing tone that the Captain murmured:

" Easy, Jewel Bright! Easy, now! Helm steady, and stand by!"

There was a moment of troubled silence; and then the old minister, clearing his throat, spoke in his gentle, tranquil voice. " My dear child," he said, " a very strange thing has come to pass; but what seems strange to us is doubtless clear and simple to the Infinite Wisdom above us. You have been a faithful and loving child, little Star, to your beloved guardian and friend here, and no father could have cared for you more tenderly than he has done. But the tie of blood is a strong one, my dear, and should not be lightly set aside. This lady is your own near relation, the sister of your dear dead mother. Through the merciful providence of God, she has been led to you, and she feels it her duty to claim you, in the name of your parents. We have considered the matter carefully, and we all feel that it is right that you should hereafter make your home with her and your uncle. This may be painful to you, my dear; but you are a good and intelligent child, and you will understand that if we give you pain now, it is to secure your future good and happiness."

He paused; and all eyes, save those keen blue ones which were studying so carefully the texture of the battered woollen cap, turned anxiously on the child. A deep flush passed over Star's face; then vanished, leaving it deadly pale, a mask of ivory with eyes of flame. When she spoke, it was in a low, suppressed voice, wholly unlike her own.

" You may kill me," said the child, " and take my body away, if you like. I will not go while I am alive."

She turned her eyes from one to the other, as if watching for the slightest motion to approach her.

Mrs. Morton, in great distress, spoke next. " My darling, it grieves me to the heart to take you from your dear, kind Daddy. But think, my Star; you are a child now, but you will soon be a woman. You cannot grow up to womanhood in a place like this. You must be with your own people, and have companions of your own age. My children will be like your own sisters and brothers. My dear, if you could only know how they will love you, how we shall all cherish and care for you!"

"When I am dead?" asked Star. "It will make no difference to me, your love, for I shall be dead. I will not go alive."

"Oh, Captain January!" cried Mrs. Morton, turning to the old man with clasped hands. "Speak to her! she will listen to you. Tell her — tell her what you said to me. Tell her that it is right for her to go; that you wish her to go!"

The old man's breathing was heavy and laboured, and for a moment it seemed as if he strove in vain for utterance: but when he spoke, his voice was still soothing and cheerful, though his whole great frame was trembling like a withered leaf. "Star Bright," he said (and between almost every word he paused to draw the short, heavy breath), "I always told ye, ye 'member, that ye was the child of gentlefolks. So bein', 'tis but right that you should have gentle raisin' by them as is yer own flesh and blood. You've done your duty, and more than your duty, by me. Now 'tis time ye did your duty by them as the Lord has sent to ye. You'll have — my — my respeckful love and duty wherever you go, my dear, and you growin' up to be a beautiful lady, as has been a little wild lass. And you'll not forget the old Cap'n, well I know, as will be very comf'table here — "

But here the child broke out with a wild, loud cry, which made all the others start to their feet. "Do you want me to go?" she cried. "Look at me, Daddy Captain! you *shall* look at me!" She snatched the cap from his hands and flung it into the fire, then faced him with blazing eyes and quivering lip. "Do you want me to go? Are you tired of me?"

Heavier and heavier grew that weight on Captain January's chest: shorter and harder came his breath. His eyes met the child's for a moment, then wavered and fell. "Why — honey — " he said, slowly, "I — I'm an old man now — a very old man. And — and — an old man likes quiet, ye see: and — I'd be quieter by myself, like; and — and so, honey — I — I'd like ye to go."

"*You lie!*" cried the child; and her voice rang like a silver trumpet in the startled ears of the listeners. "You lie to me, and you lie to God: and you *know* you lie!"

The next moment she had sprung on to the low window-sill, then turned for an instant, with her little hands clenched in menace, and her great eyes flashing fire that fell like a burning touch on every heart. Her fantastic dress gleamed like a fiery cloud against the gray outside: her hair fell like a glory about her vivid, shining face. A moment she stood there, a vision, a flying star, trailing angry light, never to be forgotten by those who saw; then, like a flash, she vanished.

Captain January tottered to his old chair and sat down in it. "The child is right, Lady and Gentleman!" he said. "I lied! I lied to my God, and to the little child who loved me. May God and the child forgive me!" And he hid his face in his hands, and silence fell for a moment.

Then Mr. Morton, who had walked hastily to the window, and was doing something with his handkerchief, beckoned to his wife. "Isabel," he said, in a low tone, "I will not be a party to this. It's an atrocious and vindictive outrage. I — I — you are not the woman I took you for, if you say another word to that old angel. Let him have the child, and send him one or two of your own into the bar—" but Isabel Morton, laughing through her tears, laid her hand over her husband's lips for a moment. Then going to the old man's chair, she knelt down by it, and took his two hands in hers.

"Captain January!" she said, tenderly. "Dear, dear Captain January! the lie is forgiven: I am very, very sure it is forgiven in heaven, as it will be forgiven in the child's loving heart. And may God never pardon me, if ever word or look of mine come again between you and the child whom God gave you!"

The gray evening was closing in around the lighthouse tower. The guests were gone, and Captain January sat alone beside the fire in his old armchair. The window was still open, for the air was soft and mild. The old man's hands were clasped upon his knee; his heart was lifted as high as heaven, in silent prayer and praise.

Suddenly, at the window, there was a gleam of yellow, a flitting shape, a look, a pause; then a great glad cry, and Star flitted like a ray of moonlight through the window, and fell on Captain January's breast.

" Daddy," she said, breaking the long, happy silence, " dear Daddy, I am sorry I burned your horrid old cap!"

CHAPTER VI.

THE SIGNAL

QUIETLY passed the days, the weeks, the months, in the lonely tower on the rock fronting the Atlantic surge. Winter came, and folded it in a white mantle, and decked it with frost-jewels. Like a pillar of ice, the tower shone in the keen brilliance of the northern sun; but within was always summer, the summer of perfect peace and contentment. To the child Star, winter was always a season of great delight; for Captain January had little to occupy him out-of-doors, and could devote much of his time to her. So there were long, delightful "jack-knife times," as Star called them, when the Captain sat fashioning all sorts of wonderful trifles with his magic knife, the child sitting at his elbow and watching him with happy eyes. There were "story times," instituted years before, as soon as Star had learned to sew on patchwork; for as for sewing *without* a story to listen to, "*that*," said Star, "is against my nature, Daddy. And you don't want me to do things that are against my nature, do you?"

So whenever the squares of gay calico came out, and the golden head bent to and fro over them, like a paradise bird hovering over a bed of gaudy flowers, the story came out, too, between puffs of the pipe, while the fire crackled a cheery accompaniment, sputtering defiance to the wind that whistled ouside. Some tale of the southern seas, and the wild tropic islands, of coral reefs and pearl-fisheries, sharks and devil-fish ; or else a whaling story, fresh and breezy as the north, full of icebergs, and seal-hunts over the cracking floes, polar bears, and all the wild delights of whale-fishing.

Then, on fine days (and oh, but the days are fine, in these glorious northern winters !) there was much joy to be had out-of-doors. For there was a spot in the little meadow, — once of gold-flecked emerald, now of spotless pearl, — a spot where the ground "tilted," to use Star's expression, suddenly down to a tiny hollow, where a fairy spring bubbled out of the rock into a fairy lake. In summer, Star rather despised this lake, which was, truth to tell, only twenty feet long and ten feet wide. It was very nice for Imogen to drink from and to stand in on hot days, and it did many lovely things in the way of reflecting blue skies and fleecy clouds and delicate traceries of leaf and bough ; but as water, it seemed a very trifling thing to a child who had the whole sweep of the Atlantic to fill her eyes, and who had the breakers for her playfellows and gossips.

But in winter, matters were different. All the

laughing lips of ripples, all the white tossing crests of waves, must content themselves with the ice-bound rocks, till spring should bring them their child-comrade again; and the little sheet of dark crystal in the hollow of the meadow had things all its own way, and mirrored back her bright face every day. The little red sled, launched at the top of the "tilt," came skimming down the slope, and shot like an arrow over the smooth ice, kept always clear of snow by the Captain's ever-busy hands; or else, when tired of coasting, the child would plant her small feet wide apart, and slide, and run, and slide again, till the pond could have cracked with pleasure, if such a thing had been in accordance with its principles.

But of all the joyous hours, none was more welcome to the child than that after the simple supper was cleared away and the room "redded up." Then, while fire and lamplight made their merriest cheer, the table was drawn up to the warmest spot; Star took her place upon Captain January's knee, and the two heads, the silver one and the golden, bent in absorbed interest over "Willum Shakespeare" or the Good Book.

Generally the Captain read aloud, but sometimes they read the parts in turn; and again sometimes the child would break off, and recite whole passages alone, with a fire and pathos which might have been that of Maid Marjorie, swaying at her childish will the heart of Sir Walter and his friends.

So quietly, in the unbroken peace which love brightened into joy, the winter passed.

At Christmas, they had, as usual, a visit from the faithful Bob, who brought all his many pockets full of candy and oranges and all manner of " truck," as he called it, for Missy Star. Also he brought a letter and a box directed only to " Captain January's Star." The letter, which the child opened with wondering eagerness, being the first she had ever received, was from Mrs. Morton. It was full of tender and loving words, wishes for Christmas cheer and New Year blessing, and with it was a photograph of the beautiful face, with its soft and tender eyes, which Star remembered so well. On the back was written, " For Little Star, from Aunt Isabel." And the box ? Why, that was quite as wonderful in its way. For it contained a most beautiful pipe for the Captain, of sweet brier-wood, mounted in silver; and oh ! oh ! such a doll ! Other children have seen such dolls, but Star never had ; a blue-eyed waxen beauty, with fringed lashes that opened and shut, rose-leaf cheeks, and fabulous wealth of silky flaxen curls. Also it had a blue velvet-frock, and its underclothing was a wonder to behold ; and the box was full of other frocks and garments.

Star took the doll in her arms with delighted awe, and seemed for a few moments absorbed in her new treasure. Presently, however, a shadow crossed her bright face. She glanced at Bob and the Captain,

and seeing that they were both engaged in busy talk,
she quietly went up to her own room, carrying the
doll with her. Here she did a strange thing. She
crossed the room to the corner where Mrs. Neptune
sat, with her back rigid, protesting against circum-
stances, and set the radiant stranger down beside her;
then, with her hands clasped behind her, and brows
bent, she considered the pair long and attentively.
Truly they were a strange contrast: the delicate,
glowing, velvet-clad doll, and the battered old wooden
image, with eyes of snail-shells and hair of brown
sea-moss. But when Star had finished her scrutiny,
she took the beautiful doll, and buried it deep under
velvets and satins at the very bottom of the great
chest. This done, she kissed Mrs. Neptune solemnly,
and proceeded to adorn her with a gorgeous Eastern
scarf, the very gayest her treasure-house could afford.

Meanwhile, in the room below, the talk went on,
grave and earnest. Troubled it was, too, on one side;
for though the Captain sat quietly in his chair, and
spoke in his usual cheerful voice, Bob Peet's rough
tones were harsh and broken, and he rose from his
place once or twice and moved uneasily about the
room.

"Cap'n," he said, " 'tain't so. Don't tell me!
Strong man — hearty — live twenty years yet —
like's not thirty! Uncle o' mine — Punksquid —
hundred and three — peart's chicken."

Captain January puffed at his pipe in silence for

some minutes. "Bob," he said, presently, "it ain't always as it's given to a man to know his time. I've allers thought I should take it particular kind if it 'corded with the Lord's views to let me know when He was ready for me. And now that He *has* let me know, and moreover has set my mind that easy about the child that it's a pleasure to think of, why, it ain't likely I shall take it anyway *but* kind. Thankin' you all the same, Bob, as have been a good mate to me, and as I sha'n't forget wherever I am. But see now!" he added, hastily, hearing a sound in the room above. "You understand, Bob; I h'ist that signal, as it might be to-morrow, and I keep her flyin' night and day. And so long as you see her flyin', you says, 'Cap'n's all right so far!' you says. But you keep a sharp lookout; and if some mornin' you don't see her, you says, 'Sailin' orders!' you says, and then you calls Cap'n Nazro, as never failed in a kindness yet, nor ain't likely to, to take the wheel, and you put for this island. And Cap'n Nazro he takes the *Huntress* in, and then goes straightway and sends a telegraft to the lady and gentleman, sayin' as Cap'n January has sailin' orders, and they please to come and take the child, as lawfully to them belongs. And you, Bob, —" the old man's steady voice faltered a little, as he laid his hand on the other's arm, — "you'll do all you can, well I know. For she'll take it hard, ye see. She has that depth o' love in her little heart, and never nobody *to* love 'cept me since she were a baby, that she'll take it cruel hard. But the Lord'll have her in mind! He'll have her in mind! and you'll stand by, Bob, and bear a hand till the lady and gentleman come."

Bob Peet held out his honest brown hand, and the two men shook hands with a certain solemnity; but before either of them could speak again, Star came singing down the stairs, and summoned them both to play at ball with oranges.

And so it came to pass that a little blue signal was hoisted at the top of the white tower, and fluttered there bravely in sun and wind. And every time the *Huntress* went thundering by (which was twice a week at this season instead of every day), Bob Peet looked out anxiously from the wheel-house window, and seeing the little banner, took cheer, and rubbed his hands and said, " Cap'n's all right so far ! "

And Captain January, whenever there came the clutch and stab at his heart, and the struggle for breath, which he had felt for the first time that September day (but ah! how many times since, and with what increasing persistence !) would creep to the stairway beside which hung the signal lines, and lay his hand on them, and wait: then, when the spasm passed, would pass his hand across his face and humbly say, " Whenever it seems right, Lord! A step nearer ! and Thou havin' the child in mind," and so go cheerfully about his work again.

There were not many more steps to take. Spring

came, and the little meadow was green again. Robins and bluebirds fluttered above the great pine-tree, and swallows built their nests under the eaves of the tower itself. The child Star sang with the birds, and danced with the dancing leaves, all unconscious of what was coming; but the old Captain's steps grew slower and heavier, day by day, and the cheery voice grew feeble, and lost its hearty ring, though never its cheeriness. " I'll set here in the porch, Jewel Bright," he would say, when the child begged him to come for a scramble on the rocks. " I think I'll jest set here, where I can see ye an' hear to ye. I'm gittin' lazy, Star Light; that's the truth. Yer old Daddy's gittin' lazy, and it's comf'tabler settin' here in the sun, than scramblin' round the rocks."

And Star would fling herself on his neck, and scold and caress him, and then go off with a half-sense of disappointment to her play. Very, very careful Captain January had to be, lest the child should suspect that which he was determined to keep from her to the last. Sometimes he half thought she must suspect, so tender was she in these days; so thoughtful, so mindful of his lightest wish. But " 'tis only the woman growin' up in her," he decided; and looking back, he remembered that she had not once broken his pipe (as she had been used to do every three or four weeks, in her sudden rages) since last September.

At last there came a day when the Captain did not even go out to the porch. It was a lovely May morning, bright and soft, with wreaths of silvery fog floating up from the blue water, and much sweet sound of singing birds and lapping waves in the air. Making some pretence of work at his carpenter's bench, the old man sent Star out to loose the cow and lead her to the water; and when she was gone, he tottered to his old chair and sat down heavily. There was no pain now, only a strange numbness, a creeping coldness, a ringing in the ears. If it might "seem right" to let him wait till the *Huntress* came by! "It's nearly time," he said, half aloud. "Nearly time, and 'twould be easier for the child."

At this moment, through the open doorway, came the silver sound of Star's voice. "But I don't think there can be any harm in my just telling you a little about it, Imogen. And the floor is the paved work of a sapphire: sapphire is a stone, just like the water over there, in the bluest place, and oh! so clear and bright, Daddy says. He saw one once. And there will be most beautiful music, Imogen. Oh! you can't think what lovely music Daddy Captain will play on a harp. I know he will, 'cause he will be a spirit of just men made perfect: and that will be a *great* thing, Imogen; for he has never known how to play on anything before: and — " Ah! the sweet, childish prattle! but already it was growing faint upon the old man's ears.

"Star Bright!" he called; and the dancing shape came flying, and stood on tiptoe in the doorway.

Steady, now, January! keep your voice steady, if there is any will left in you. Keep your head turned a little away, lest there be any change in your face, yet not turned enough to make her wonder. "Star Bright," said Captain January, "it's about — time — for the *Huntress* — to be along, isn't it?"

"Yes, Daddy," said the child; "she's just in sight now. Shall I go down and wave to Bob as he goes by?"

"Yes, Honeysuckle," said the old man. "And — and wait to see if he comes ashore. I think — likely — Bob'll come ashore to-day. He was goin' to bring — somethin' — for me. Is there a squall comin' up, Jewel Bright?"

"A squall, Daddy?" said the child, wondering. "Why, there isn't a cloud in the sky."

"Jes' so!" said Captain January. "I — only jist asked. Good-bye, Star Bright."

"Dear Daddy! Good-bye!" cried the child, and she sped away over the rocks.

So dark! and not a cloud in the sky. If he might have looked once more, with those fast-darkening eyes, at the little blessed face which held all the world in it! if he could call her back now, and kiss her once more, and hold her little hand — No! no! steady, January! steady now, and stand by!

Quite dark now. But that does not matter. No need of light for what is now to be done. Slowly the old man raises himself; feels for the wall, creeps along beside it. Here is the line. Is there any strength left in that benumbed arm? Yes! "For the child, dear Lord, and Thou helpin' me, as ever has been!"

Down comes the signal, and the old man creeps back to his chair again, and composes himself decently, with reverent, folded hands, and head bowed in waiting. "'He holdeth the waters in the hollow of His hand. Behold, He taketh up the isles as a very little thing.' Amen! so be it!"

Wave, little Star! wave your little blue apron from the rocks, and laugh and clap your hands for pleasure, as the ripples from the steamer's bow break in snowy foam at your feet. Bend to your oar, Bob Peet, and send your little black boat flying over the water as she never flew before! and press on, friendly *Huntress*, to your port, whence the winged message may speed on its way to the stately lady with the tender eyes, who waits for tidings in her distant home.

For Captain January's last voyage is over, and he is already in the haven where he would be.

THE END.

Selections from The Page Company's Books for Young People

THE BLUE BONNET SERIES

Each large 12mo, cloth decorative, illustrated, per volume **$1.50**

A TEXAS BLUE BONNET
By Caroline E. Jacobs.

"The book's heroine, Blue Bonnet, has the very finest kind of wholesome, honest, lively girlishness."—*Chicago Inter-Ocean.*

BLUE BONNET'S RANCH PARTY
By Caroline E. Jacobs and Edyth Ellerbeck Read.

"A healthy, natural atmosphere breathes from every chapter."—*Boston Transcript.*

BLUE BONNET IN BOSTON; Or, Boarding-School Days at Miss North's.
By Caroline E. Jacobs and Lela Horn Richards.

"It is bound to become popular because of its wholesomeness and its many human touches."—*Boston Globe.*

BLUE BONNET KEEPS HOUSE; Or, The New Home in the East.
By Caroline E. Jacobs and Lela Horn Richards.

"It cannot fail to prove fascinating to girls in their teens."—*New York Sun.*

BLUE BONNET—DÉBUTANTE
By Lela Horn Richards.

An interesting picture of the unfolding of life for Blue Bonnet.

A—1

THE YOUNG PIONEER SERIES

By Harrison Adams

Each 12mo, cloth decorative, illustrated, per volume **$1.25**

THE PIONEER BOYS OF THE OHIO; Or, Clearing the Wilderness.

" Such books as this are an admirable means of stimulating among the young Americans of to-day interest in the story of their pioneer ancestors and the early days of the Republic." — *Boston Globe.*

THE PIONEER BOYS ON THE GREAT LAKES; Or, On the Trail of the Iroquois.

" The recital of the daring deeds of the frontier is not only interesting but instructive as well and shows the sterling type of character which these days of self-reliance and trial produced." — *American Tourist, Chicago.*

THE PIONEER BOYS OF THE MISSISSIPPI; Or, The Homestead in the Wilderness.

"The story is told with spirit, and is full of adventure."—*New York Sun.*

THE PIONEER BOYS OF THE MISSOURI; Or, In the Country of the Sioux.

" Vivid in style, vigorous in movement, full of dramatic situations, true to historic perspective, this story is a capital one for boys."—*Watchman Examiner, New York City.*

THE PIONEER BOYS OF THE YELLOWSTONE; Or, Lost in the Land of Wonders.

" There is plenty of lively adventure and action and the story is well told."—*Duluth Herald, Duluth, Minn.*

THE PIONEER BOYS OF THE COLUMBIA; Or, In the Wilderness of the Great Northwest.

" The story is full of spirited action and contains much valuable historical information."—*Boston Herald.*

A—2

THE HADLEY HALL SERIES
By Louise M. Breitenbach

Each large 12mo, cloth decorative, illustrated, per volume **$1.50**

ALMA AT HADLEY HALL
"The author is to be congratulated on having written such an appealing book for girls." — *Detroit Free Press.*

ALMA'S SOPHOMORE YEAR
"It cannot fail to appeal to the lovers of good things in girls' books." — *Boston Herald.*

ALMA'S JUNIOR YEAR
"The diverse characters in the boarding-school are strongly drawn, the incidents are well developed and the action is never dull." — *The Boston Herald.*

ALMA'S SENIOR YEAR
"Incident abounds in all of Miss Breitenbach's stories and a healthy, natural atmosphere breathes from every chapter." — *Boston Transcript.*

THE GIRLS OF FRIENDLY TERRACE SERIES
By Harriet Lummis Smith

Each large 12mo, cloth decorative, illustrated, per volume **$1.50**

THE GIRLS OF FRIENDLY TERRACE
"A book sure to please girl readers, for the author seems to understand perfectly the girl character." — *Boston Globe.*

PEGGY RAYMOND'S VACATION
"It is a wholesome, hearty story."—*Utica Observer.*

PEGGY RAYMOND'S SCHOOL DAYS
The book is delightfully written, and contains lots of exciting incidents.

A—3

FAMOUS LEADERS SERIES

By CHARLES H. L. JOHNSTON

Each large 12mo, cloth decorative, illustrated, per volume **$1.50**

FAMOUS CAVALRY LEADERS

" More of such books should be written, books that acquaint young readers with historical personages in a pleasant, informal way." — *New York Sun.*

" It is a book that will stir the heart of every boy and will prove interesting as well to the adults." — *Lawrence Daily World.*

FAMOUS INDIAN CHIEFS

" Mr. Johnston has done faithful work in this volume, and his relation of battles, sieges and struggles of these famous Indians with the whites for the possession of America is a worthy addition to United States History." — *New York Marine Journal.*

FAMOUS SCOUTS

" It is the kind of a book that will have a great fascination for boys and young men, and while it entertains them it will also present valuable information in regard to those who have left their impress upon the history of the country." — *The New London Day.*

FAMOUS PRIVATEERSMEN AND ADVEN-TURERS OF THE SEA

" The tales are more than merely interesting; they are entrancing, stirring the blood with thrilling force and bringing new zest to the never-ending interest in the dramas of the sea." — *The Pittsburgh Post.*

FAMOUS FRONTIERSMEN AND HEROES OF THE BORDER

" The accounts are not only authentic, but distinctly readable, making a book of wide appeal to all who love the history of actual adventure." — *Cleveland Leader.*

FAMOUS DISCOVERERS AND EXPLORERS OF AMERICA

" The book is an epitome of some of the wildest and bravest adventures of which the world has known and of discoveries which have changed the face of the old world as well as of the new." — *Brooklyn Daily Eagle.*

A—4

HILDEGARDE - MARGARET SERIES

By LAURA E. RICHARDS

Eleven Volumes

The Hildegarde-Margaret Series, beginning with "Queen Hildegarde" and ending with "The Merryweathers," make one of the best and most popular series of books for girls ever written.

Each large 12mo, cloth decorative, illustrated, per volume $1.35
The eleven volumes boxed as a set . . . $14.85

LIST OF TITLES

QUEEN HILDEGARDE

HILDEGARDE'S HOLIDAY

HILDEGARDE'S HOME

HILDEGARDE'S NEIGHBORS

HILDEGARDE'S HARVEST

THREE MARGARETS

MARGARET MONTFORT

PEGGY

RITA

FERNLEY HOUSE

THE MERRYWEATHERS
A—5

THE CAPTAIN JANUARY SERIES

By Laura E. Richards

Each one volume, 12mo, cloth decorative, illustrated, per volume   60 cents

CAPTAIN JANUARY

A charming idyl of New England coast life, whose success has been very remarkable.

SAME. *Illustrated Holiday Edition* . . $1.35

MELODY: The Story of a Child.

MARIE

A companion to "Melody" and "Captain January."

ROSIN THE BEAU

A sequel to "Melody" and "Marie."

SNOW-WHITE; Or, The House in the Wood.

JIM OF HELLAS; Or, In Durance Vile, and a companion story, Bethesda Pool.

NARCISSA

And a companion story, In Verona, being two delightful short stories of New England life.

"SOME SAY"

And a companion story, Neighbors in Cyrus.

NAUTILUS

"'Nautilus' is by far the best product of the author's powers, and is certain to achieve the wide success it so richly merits."

ISLA HERON

This interesting story is written in the author's usual charming manner.

THE LITTLE MASTER

"A well told, interesting tale of a high character." — *California Gateway Gazette.*

A—6

DELIGHTFUL BOOKS FOR LITTLE FOLKS

By LAURA E. RICHARDS

THREE MINUTE STORIES

Cloth decorative, 12mo, with eight plates in full color
and many text illustrations $1.35
"Little ones will understand and delight in the stories
and poems." — *Indianapolis News.*

FIVE MINUTE STORIES

Cloth decorative, square 12mo, illustrated . $1.35
A charming collection of short stories and clever poems
for children.

MORE FIVE MINUTE STORIES

Cloth decorative, square 12mo, illustrated . $1.35
A noteworthy collection of short stories and poems
for children, which will prove as popular with mothers
as with boys and girls.

FIVE MICE IN A MOUSE TRAP

Cloth decorative, square 12mo, illustrated . $1.35
The story of their lives and other wonderful things
related by the Man in the Moon, done in the vernacular
from the lunacular form by Laura E. Richards.

POLLYANNA ANNUAL NO. 1

Trade Mark
The Yearly GLAD Book.
Trade ——— Mark
Edited by FLORENCE ORVILLE.
Large octavo, with nearly 200 illustrations, 12 in full
color, bound with an all-over pictorial cover design in
colors, with fancy printed end papers. $1.50

"The contents of this splendid volume are evidently
intended to demonstrate the fact that work is as good
a glad game as play if gone about the right way. There
are clever little drawings any one could imitate, and in
imitating learn something. There are adventurous tales,
fairy tales, scientific tales, comic stories and serious
stories in verse and prose." — *Montreal Herald and Star.*
A—7

THE LITTLE COLONEL BOOKS
(Trade Mark)

By ANNIE FELLOWS JOHNSTON

Each large 12mo, cloth, illustrated, per volume . **$1.50**

THE LITTLE COLONEL STORIES
(Trade Mark)

Being three " Little Colonel " stories in the Cosy Corner Series, " The Little Colonel," " Two Little Knights of Kentucky," and " The Giant Scissors," in a single volume.

THE LITTLE COLONEL'S HOUSE PARTY
(Trade Mark)

THE LITTLE COLONEL'S HOLIDAYS
(Trade Mark)

THE LITTLE COLONEL'S HERO
(Trade Mark)

THE LITTLE COLONEL AT BOARDING-
(Trade Mark)
SCHOOL

THE LITTLE COLONEL IN ARIZONA
(Trade Mark)

THE LITTLE COLONEL'S CHRISTMAS
(Trade Mark)
VACATION

THE LITTLE COLONEL, MAID OF HONOR
(Trade Mark)

THE LITTLE COLONEL'S KNIGHT COMES
(Trade Mark)
RIDING

THE LITTLE COLONEL'S CHUM, MARY
WARE (Trade Mark)

MARY WARE IN TEXAS

MARY WARE'S PROMISED LAND

These twelve volumes, boxed as a set, $18.00.

A—9

SPECIAL HOLIDAY EDITIONS

Each small quarto, cloth decorative, per volume . **$1.35**
New plates, handsomely illustrated with eight full-page drawings in color, and many marginal sketches.

THE LITTLE COLONEL
(Trade Mark)

TWO LITTLE KNIGHTS OF KENTUCKY

THE GIANT SCISSORS

BIG BROTHER

THE JOHNSTON JEWEL SERIES

Each small 16mo, cloth decorative, with frontispiece and decorative text borders, per volume **$0.60**

IN THE DESERT OF WAITING: THE LEGEND OF CAMELBACK MOUNTAIN.

THE THREE WEAVERS: A FAIRY TALE FOR FATHERS AND MOTHERS AS WELL AS FOR THEIR DAUGHTERS.

KEEPING TRYST: A TALE OF KING ARTHUR'S TIME.

THE LEGEND OF THE BLEEDING HEART

THE RESCUE OF PRINCESS WINSOME: A FAIRY PLAY FOR OLD AND YOUNG.

THE JESTER'S SWORD

THE LITTLE COLONEL'S GOOD TIMES BOOK

Uniform in size with the Little Colonel Series . **$1.50**
Bound in white kid (morocco) and gold . **3.00**
Cover design and decorations by Peter Verberg.
"A mighty attractive volume in which the owner may record the good times she has on decorated pages, and under the directions as it were of Annie Fellows Johnston." — *Buffalo Express.*

A—10

THE LITTLE COLONEL DOLL BOOK — First Series

Quarto, boards, printed in colors . . . $1.50
A series of "Little Colonel" dolls. Each has several changes of costume, so they can be appropriately clad for the rehearsal of any scene or incident in the series.

THE LITTLE COLONEL DOLL BOOK — Second Series

Quarto, boards, printed in colors . . . $1.50
An artistic series of paper dolls, including not only lovable Mary Ware, the Little Colonel's chum, but many another of the much loved characters which appear in the last three volumes of the famous "Little Colonel Series."

ASA HOLMES

By ANNIE FELLOWS JOHNSTON.
With a frontispiece by Ernest Fosbery.
16mo, cloth decorative, gilt top . . . $1.00
"'Asa Holmes' is the most delightful, most sympathetic and wholesome book that has been published in a long while." — *Boston Times.*

TRAVELERS FIVE: ALONG LIFE'S HIGHWAY

By ANNIE FELLOWS JOHNSTON.
With an introduction by Bliss Carman, and a frontispiece by E. H. Garrett.
12mo, cloth decorative $1.25
" Mrs. Johnston broadens her reputation with this book so rich in the significance of common things." — *Boston Advertiser.*

JOEL: A BOY OF GALILEE

By ANNIE FELLOWS JOHNSTON.
12mo, cloth decorative, illustrated . . . $1.50
" The book is a very clever handling of the greatest event in the history of the world." — *Rochester, N. Y., Herald.*

A—11

THE BOYS' STORY OF THE ARMY SERIES

By Florence Kimball Russel

BORN TO THE BLUE

12mo, cloth decorative, illustrated . . . $1.50

"The story deserves warm commendation and genuine popularity."—*Army and Navy Register.*

IN WEST POINT GRAY

12mo, cloth decorative, illustrated . . . $1.50

"One of the best books that deals with West Point."—*New York Sun.*

FROM CHEVRONS TO SHOULDER-STRAPS

12mo, cloth decorative, illustrated . . . $1.50

"The life of a cadet at West Point is portrayed very realistically."—*The Hartford Post, Hartford, Conn.*

DOCTOR'S LITTLE GIRL SERIES

By Marion Ames Taggart

Each large 12mo, cloth, illustrated, per volume, $1.50

THE DOCTOR'S LITTLE GIRL

"A charming story of the ups and downs of the life of a dear little maid."—*The Churchman.*

SWEET NANCY: The Further Adventures of the Doctor's Little Girl.

"Just the sort of book to amuse, while its influence cannot but be elevating."—*New York Sun.*

NANCY, THE DOCTOR'S LITTLE PARTNER

"The story is sweet and fascinating, such as many girls of wholesome tastes will enjoy."—*Springfield Union.*

NANCY PORTER'S OPPORTUNITY

"Nancy shows throughout that she is a splendid young woman, with plenty of pluck."—*Boston Globe.*

NANCY AND THE COGGS TWINS

"The story is refreshing."—*New York Sun.*

A—12